Jinx or not, he intended to have her

Callie writhed in Rock's grasp, demanding, "Just what the devil do you think you're doing?"

His answer was to lower her to the floor of the hayloft and pull her T-shirt over her head. "You are the most beautiful woman…" he muttered in awe.

Her brain fogged as he caressed the rounded fullness of her breasts. She gasped and tried to get control of her runaway response when he took one nipple into his mouth.

Then he took her hand and placed it on the straining placket of his jeans and she felt his arousal.

Her touch was too much. Rock's breathing sounded like a freight train struggling uphill. "Callie, I want you… And now, at long last…" He gasped, pulling his straining zipper down.

His bare chest heaved as he stood on one leg and struggled to pull off a boot. Never taking his eyes from Callie, he hopped around off balance, tugging at the other stubborn boot. One more hop to the right and the boot slid from his foot.

And then Rock disappeared through the floor….

D1012408

Heather Warren knows all about cowboys. She lives and works on a dairy farm with her husband and two daughters in the cottage country area of Ontario, Canada. A self-professed readaholic, Heather quickly became hooked on romance fiction. She started penning her own stories some fourteen years ago. Still believing that love really does make the world go round and that humor is an integral part of any relationship, she wrote *Head Over Spurs*—her first Temptation novel and a delightful romp.

HEAD OVER SPURS
Heather Warren

Harlequin Books

TORONTO • NEW YORK • LONDON
AMSTERDAM • PARIS • SYDNEY • HAMBURG
STOCKHOLM • ATHENS • TOKYO • MILAN
MADRID • WARSAW • BUDAPEST • AUCKLAND

For Robert who weathers the ups and downs on the roller coaster of living with a writer. And for Susan who pushed, prodded, guided and hammered things into my stubborn head. My eternal thanks.

ISBN 0-373-25767-8

HEAD OVER SPURS

1

"THE TWO OF YOU need to get married," Roarke McCall grumbled, his back turned on the sight of his two younger brothers. He noted with satisfaction that the room had stilled to a deathly silence. "At least then you can work out your overzealous hormones in bed with your wives."

"Ah, hell," Rock uttered, the disgust evident in his voice. "What the hell are you trying to pull Roarke? How the heck are we supposed to get married when neither of us has a girl?" His heavy crockery mug slammed to the table. Coffee sloshed over the rim, ran down the worn length of the table and dribbled to the floor unheeded. "Not that I wouldn't enjoy having a woman warm my bed every night." Rock leaned back to balance on the rear legs of his chair and smirked, then cast a doubtful glance toward his brother. "But I think you're barking up the wrong tree."

Roarke turned to face the battered twosome. "Well, things are going to have to change around here. I can't take much more of these stupid barroom brawls. And I don't fancy pouring our hard-earned profits into Klancey's bar to pay for the damages. Seems like every damn weekend there's a ruckus down there, and one of you guys are at the bottom of it. Why can't you both just go have a drink and flirt a little instead of this insanity? It's time that you straightened your lives out. You're supposed to be mature adults by now, with common sense."

After a long sip of coffee, he took in the spectacle the two of them made and frowned. Rock was sporting a black eye, the same one that had already been blackened three times this spring, and it was only April. An angry crimson gash traveled the edge of his sharply contoured cheek. It was swollen, but went well with his split lip.

Roarke shook his head as his gaze shifted to Reese. Strong silent Reese, who'd never gotten into this kind of trouble until lately. Both his eyes were bloodshot, the left nearly swollen shut. The bruising that fanned out into his hairline looked purple and tender. He was favoring his right side this morning, and Roarke knew damned well why. He'd seen the bruises forming last night when he'd helped him into bed. He wouldn't be surprised if he had a couple of cracked ribs.

Reese winced painfully as he rose to his feet. "Count me out. Women are nothing but trouble. How the hell do you think it got started last night?"

They stared curiously at Reese as he wandered slowly to the stove, flinching as he poured coffee and returned to the table. Supporting his bruised ribs, he maneuvered himself into his chair with the utmost care. He glanced at his brothers, then sighed heavily. "Ah, forget it."

Roarke and Rock glanced at each other thoughtfully and let the subject drop. Even at the best of times

Reese didn't talk much. Perhaps this was one time when it wasn't worth pushing him.

They ate in silence until Rock rose to his feet and crossed to the old blackened range to get more coffee. "Now that I think about it, maybe your notion isn't so bad, Roarke. It might be a good idea. Maybe we all need to get married, including you. It's been a long time since Blue Sky Ranch has seen a woman on its land. But you'll notice that I said *all* of us."

"I'm too old for a wife. Hell, I'm forty-one next month and too set in my ways." Roarke grumbled around the eggs he'd shoveled into his mouth.

"Yeah, but you still like a little filly in your bed once in a while. We've heard all the gossip." Rock returned to his chair and flopped down. "Seems you've got quite the reputation for keeping the ladies happy. Rumor has it that you have the magic touch." Rock chuckled bawdily. "Anyway, you're not too old. Lots of men marry late in life. Anything I've read says older men make better husbands because they know what's out there, sampled all the goods so to speak. And then they pick the best. Besides, you're more than settled now and you've got more to offer a woman than you did ten or fifteen years ago."

Reese slammed his coffee cup down and burst out, "It's all fine and dandy for you guys to talk about getting married. Assuming you can find the right woman, where the hell are we going to live with these perspective wives? This old shack isn't suitable for any woman, let alone three of them. It hasn't seen a coat of paint in years, and the furniture is so old it's falling apart. Any woman who ventured in here would turn face and run for cover." He shook his head as he glanced around the dingy little kitchen.

"Anyway, where the devil do you expect to find a woman way out here in the middle of nowhere? The half-decent women are already married, and what's left you sure as hell wouldn't want to marry."

Roarke sighed as he glanced around the kitchen. Reese had a point. The floor was worn in places, and they'd all but stopped washing it years ago. The appliances were so old it was a miracle they still ran. The kitchen counters were stained and faded, with holes that had been burned into them over the years. The wallpaper was yellowed and peeling at the ceiling and beside the door. There were two gaping holes in the wall produced by temper-induced punches. The windows were so dirty you couldn't see out of them unless you cleared a spot with the once yellow curtains that hung limp and soiled beside them. And this was the best room in the house.

"Well, we'll just have to build a couple of new houses. We can afford that. We can each choose a site and we'll get someone in to do the building. That alone will attract a woman. What woman can resist the lure of a brand-new house?" Roarke rose. "Now that's settled, let's get to work. We should go down and check out that hay in the south forty by the road, and those cows and calves should be looked at today."

"Just wait a minute." Reese's annoyed voice stopped everything. "I have something to tell you guys, and since the subject of marriage has come up, it may as well be now. I'm already married."

Silence filled the room like a lead balloon as the brothers stared at Reese, stunned and almost unbelieving. "When? Who?"

Reese shook his head slowly and sipped at his coffee. "Melody Collier, just after we graduated from college."

"Well, for pete's sake, that's been years. What's going on?" Roarke demanded, as if they had the right to know.

"We married because we've always been in love, but Melody really wanted to go and see if she could make it as a singer. We agreed she'd have seven years to search out her future. We've kept in contact and seen each other often enough. But I guess we've grown apart over the years. Time will tell if we have what it takes to pull things together again. Still, I wouldn't mind the new house. I think Melody would like to come home to someplace comfortable we can call our own."

The brothers sat in shocked silence. Reese continued, "I think Rock's got a point, Roarke. If he has to find a wife then so do you, and don't go spouting that garbage about being old. Look at Pete Butter. He was older than you are when he got married. He has three kids now and he's doing just fine. If you insist on going through with this ridiculous scheme, then you should be included in it, too. And if you don't find a wife, Rock and I will find one for you."

Rock chuckled wickedly as he rose to his feet to lean against the counter, his arms crossed over his wide chest. "Yeah, and I know just the woman. Betty Rogers has had her eye on Roarke for years."

Reese burst into deep, belly-rumbling laughter, then grabbed at his aching ribs. Roarke cast a black scowl at his brothers. Betty Rogers was fifty if she was a day, she owned the local café and had six snotty-nosed little ankle biters from six different men. It was no secret that she was looking for a father for them. She also weighed about three hundred pounds and had a voice like an old hen being plucked alive.

"I don't think so. I've had my days of dating and love. I can do without it. I don't like the idea of changing my ways to accommodate a woman. But I still think the house idea is a good one. We're all too old to be living together."

Reese shrugged and spoke again. "So we'll each look for a site, and in the meantime, Rock, be looking for a wife. I'll work at getting Melody to come home. And you, Roarke...maybe you're right, but then maybe you're not. I think if Rock and I can manage to settle down happily, so could you," Reese stated firmly.

"Yeah, I think so, too. We'll never hold you to anything, Roarke, but it wouldn't be fair to you if Reese and I got all the fun and glory of having a wife. Maybe we'll have to find you one ourselves."

Roarke sputtered, looking dark and angry. He shook his head as he rose from the table and placed his hat on his head.

"I don't have any intention of becoming involved with your scheming. Find yourself a wife, Rock, and settle down." He glanced at Reese with a pained look. "I'll contact a friend of mine who builds log homes and see if he can send someone out to show us a few plans. Maybe that'll bring Melody home for you, Reese. As for me, don't you guys worry. I know what I'm doing with my life, and I don't need any help from anyone."

CALLIE MASTERS normally considered herself to be calm, cool and collected. But not today. She'd been on the road for ten hours and was a questionable forty miles from her destination when her truck started to cough and sputter. Her temper soared to an almost uncontrollable level.

To say that things hadn't gone well today would be a slight understatement. She was on some godforsaken road high in the mountains with no hope of help for miles.

Callie pulled onto the narrow shoulder just beyond the curve she'd barely managed to get around, then threw on her brake and killed the sickly engine. Her mood sizzled as hot as that little red light on the dash that was angrily flashing at her.

Glaring at the dashboard, her nostrils flaring with something greater than animosity toward the decrepit old truck, Callie pounded on the steering wheel. She cursed a blue streak until the flare of rage blew itself out.

Stray glossy black curls fell around her face as she laid her head on the steering wheel and counted. Not to ten or twenty or even fifty—she counted to a hundred and then counted backward to zero.

Only then did she look up to survey the area where she was stranded. Rain steadily pounded on the roof, and a mysterious dense fog surrounded her, which made her feel as if she'd been transported into another millenium. This high in the mountains, there was nothing but road, rock and dull gray fog as far as the eye could see. Other than the rain, it was silent, and there was no sign of life, human or otherwise.

She wouldn't have been here, either, if she hadn't practically asked to be sent out to the middle of nowhere. Lately she had been a little unpredictable and erratic. But her life had blown up in her face before Christmas, just when everything was supposed to be falling into place. Being left at the altar was not the road to peace and security within yourself. Callie knew her father and her two brothers were probably more upset about it than she had been. And that's why they'd dispatched her to a small town on the other side of the Rocky Mountains called Pinetar. There, she was supposed to design and build log homes for some friends of her eldest brother.

Callie knew in her heart that they had done it for her own good. She needed to get out of town, away from all the gossip and stories about her aborted wedding. But she also knew they had assigned her this job to keep her out of trouble.

It was no secret that she had been lax lately, staying out until all hours of the night. Little did her family know that most nights she ended up at the lake, sitting alone, thinking about a future that seemed pretty bleak. That is, until a couple of weeks ago when she had decided to pull up her socks and get on with life.

Callie sighed and noticed that the rain had slowed to a sprinkle. Resigned to her purgatory, she stepped out of the Jeep, went around and raised the hood, muttering graphically about the paternity of the stupid temperamental piece of junk.

"Just what I need to make this day absolutely perfect," she grumbled. She looked at the foggy, wet sky and threw up her hands. "What's wrong, did You run out of people to pick on? Why me, twice in one day?" Then, feeling ashamed, Callie shrugged and turned to the truck. She mumbled a quick apology. "I guess I should be cursing the other fellow, but darn it, couldn't You at least help a little?"

She climbed up on the front bumper, leaned over the engine and started probing just as she'd seen her brothers do a million times, although she didn't have a clue what she was doing.

She stared at the mess of tangled wires and hoses. How the devil could anyone make sense out of that mess? The dirt, oil and grease plastered all over only confused things.

She climbed down and circled the truck and camper, trying to remember what her brothers had attempted to teach her eight billion years ago about trucks and the reasons they stopped. She leaned against the old camper. There really wasn't much she could do but give in to the fact that she was defeated for the day. She'd have to wait for someone to come along. Maybe a park ranger would be able to help.

Callie kicked the tire in frustration. A loud hissing filled the air, and she watched in disbelief as the air leaked out of the tire that she'd replaced that very morning. "Oh, great, another flat tire! It goes well with the wonderful miracle vehicle I've been awarded today. Why don't we just make life real miserable for Callie Masters, shall we? Let's have a real good storm blow up now." In answer to her suggestion, thunder rumbled and icy rain began to pelt down.

Callie raced to the front of the truck and slammed the hood down. The last thing she needed was for the engine to get wet. But the momentum of the slamming pushed her off balance. The slippery clay under her feet didn't help. She landed heavily on her bottom.

This is what her father would have called a kick in the pants to smarten you up.

Sufficiently chastised, Callie pulled herself to her feet and wiped the mud from her hands on the legs of her pants. She swallowed the temper tantrum that threatened and methodically made her way around to pull the jack from the back seat. Seeing as she was already wet and dirty, she may as well try to fix the flat.

Out of sheer stubbornness and temper—or maybe it was just plain luck—she managed to get the jack placed under the trailer. The rain drenched her, and the slippery clay mud that was everywhere hampered her efforts.

Then the next source of aggravation became evident. The truck driver who had insisted on helping her this morning had tightened the wheel nuts so darn well she couldn't even begin to budge them.

Callie was at the end of her tether. She didn't want to be hauling this stupid camper all over hell's half acre, and she didn't want to be heading for a season on a ranch with three old bachelor brothers.

She was a good architect and she'd been doing a fine job on the new catalogue for the business. Masters Log Homes had a good reputation, but with this creative catalogue and her innovative designs, it would be even more prestigious. She'd been content to hide away in her office, working on the project and doing her part for the family business.

Unfortunately, Roarke McCall had phoned. Callie had fought her brothers and father on this, but they'd given her no choice. They saw it as someplace safe for her. She saw it as dull and probably boring as hell.

"Three crusty old bachelors. Out in the middle of nowhere for God only knew how long. Now why wouldn't a girl look forward to that?" Callie muttered to herself as she put all her muscle behind the lug nuts.

By the time Mr. Macho Alberta Cowboy stopped and offered her help in a condescendingly sweet tone, calling her "honey," Callie had reached her limit. She slowly rose to her feet, her hair dripping, not caring that she looked like a drowned rat. She stared him straight in the eye and very rudely told him what he could do with his honey and his offer of help.

"Whoa, baby." The stunned cowboy held his hands in front of him protectively as he backed away. "I only wanted to help, nothing else. But if you've got it all under control, far be it from me to interfere. I'll just leave the way I came." He climbed into his truck and took off like a bat out of hell.

Callie stood in awed shock as her only source of help drove off, leaving her stranded. She was stuck on top of a mountain with a truck that didn't work and a flat tire that was bolted on far too tight. And, she noticed for the first time, a spare that was as flat as the tire on there now. Tears threatened, but she was so angry at herself and the world, she refused to let them have their way.

Carefully she climbed into the cab of the truck to gather her purse. Her clothes were wet and dirty, her shoulders were heaving and her head was buzzing. It was then she noticed the gas gauge. The needle sat guiltily on empty, in fact well past empty onto dry.

That was when all hell broke loose. Callie hopped out of the truck and stood in the downpour. She paced in one direction then the other, then stopped and let out a long, blood-curdling scream of frustration.

Then she dropped to the ground and had a good cry. The rain was letting up, and the darkening sky was fast closing in around her, but she sat there and let it all out.

ROCK MCCALL was flying high. He'd had the best of times west of the mountains today—competition, horses and adoration from a good percentage of the female population. It had been the best little rodeo fair he'd been to in a while. He'd all but walked away with the top dollar in prizes. He felt great, in fact even better than great.

Belting out a good old country tune about a woman bringing out the wild side of a man, he whipped around the curve and almost rear-ended a camper at the edge of the road.

Hell, now what the devil is that doing there? Don't these stupid tourists ever think about what they're doing? Parking a vehicle at the side of the road this close to the curve has to be the most stupid move I've seen yet.

Shaking his head, he pulled over in front of an old Jeep attached to an ancient camper. He climbed out of his truck, then stopped for a second to appreciate the special silence. This far up there was nothing but the lonely sound of the wind blowing in the cloud-spattered moonlight and a few hardy insects. This was his space. He'd loved it as a kid and grown to respect it as a man.

With a heart-felt sigh, he paced around the vehicles. He found no one and saw nothing much wrong—not that he could see anything in the dark shadows. It was a matter of some cheapskate trying to get a free camping spot for the night. Mumbling and cursing at the stupidity of the owner, he pounded on the door and waited.

Callie leaped up from the table. The noise at the door had shocked her from a deep sleep. Being well past exhausted, she had decided to wait in the camper out of the rain for a ranger to come by. She'd fallen asleep after she changed out of her damp clothes and had something to eat.

Fumbling in the dark, she grasped the normally stiff handle of the door and pushed with all her strength.

For once it didn't stick.

Flying out of the camper, she landed right in the arms of a very big, very hard, very male body. She let out a small scream as she careened into him, sending

them both tumbling down a small rocky embank-
ment. Over and over they went, holding onto each
other for dear life. Grunting and groaning, they came
to a jarring stop at the bottom of the small ravine
some distance from the road.

Callie swallowed hard and listened cautiously. A
rough gasping sound above her head was all she
heard. Her shirt and jeans were wet from the roll
down the hill. And she knew from the feel of things
that she'd wear the bruises from this tumble for some
time.

Damp and tousled, she drew in a deep breath and
prepared to move. She had no idea what to say. What
in the devil had happened? One minute she was
sleeping and the next she was at the bottom of a hill
all over some man.

"Sweet Jesus and all saints." A deep resonant voice
echoed beneath her ear. Only then did Callie realize
the position she was in. Not only was her ear pressed
up against this mountain man's chest—her body was
sprawled in a very intimate manner over his. He was
a big man. From where she lay there was still another
half of a wide, muscular chest in view. And if she
wasn't mistaken, she was straddled over one of his
thick thighs. Oh, Lord.

Her nose was nestled in a deep forest of soft, dark
curls. The delicious scent of leather, horses and musk
assaulted her, turning her into mush.

Callie attempted to move, but a pair of giant im-
prisoning hands and a painful groan quickly stopped
her.

"Don't you dare move, lady. Combined with the

fact that you've single-handedly managed to knock the wind out of me, you've also done some mighty fine damage to that area where your knee is. So I think you'd better stay still until I can breathe a little easier and can move you myself," he warned roughly.

That wasn't the only problem Rock had. This time bomb who had erupted from the trailer had managed to turn his entire body into Silly Putty. Her compact but lush little body was causing some serious distress to a part of his body that did not need any extra stimulation at the moment.

It didn't take much for Rock to realize that every inch of her was woman. From the lush curves of her breasts nestled into his ribs to the slim thighs that were wrapped around one leg squeezing the life from him, he recognized prime femininity. Damn, if she didn't fit him perfectly.

Rock groaned as his bruised parts responded to her softness. Hormones flared freely despite his injuries, and his blood rushed double quick. Maybe Roarke had been right when he'd accused him of thinking with his jeans. He seemed to have no control over his lecherous thoughts at the moment, and it was damn painful.

Callie flinched, realizing the position she was in and what was happening below her. "I...I didn't— Oh, my God, I hope I didn't... Oh damn..." She moved ever so slightly and was rewarded by another groan and the tightening of his big hands on her upper arms.

Wincing, Callie froze. What in heaven's name was

she going to do? What if this guy was faking? What if he was some kind of lecher who enjoyed this kind of thing? What if she had damaged him? She lay still, praying that whoever was responsible for the day she was having was still watching her misery and would decide that enough was enough.

But it wasn't, something was however, crawling up her pant leg. Callie froze. Surely it was only her imagination. Lord knows, she'd been told often enough that she had a very vivid one. She laid perfectly still. It moved upward, then stopped. Callie waited with bated breath. A few seconds passed, and she felt the movement again, this time well past her knee and getting higher. That did it. She bounded to her feet, ignoring the cowboy's groans of protest.

Shaking her leg frantically, she couldn't dislodge whatever it was that had found its way in there and was climbing higher. Images of snakes, toads, mice filled her mind. Off came her jeans, faster than they'd ever been shed before. And in the bright, clear moonlight a small green cricket jumped from the folds of the stone-washed denim.

Breathing an audible sigh of relief, Callie held her chest as her heart slowly began to calm. Never in her life could she recall feeling as scared as she had for those few seconds. She watched as the small insect merrily hopped on its way.

A raspy chuckle followed by a harsh gasp filled the silence. Callie glanced at the stranger she'd been so intimately entwined with mere seconds ago. He lay staring at her. Shock filled her instantly. Here she stood in her white lace bikini panties, giving him a free show, and he was lapping up the sight.

"Damned if this wouldn't happen when I'm least likely to be able to enjoy it," he muttered. She was one good-looking woman. The moon reflected off the blue-black hair that curled and twisted wildly around her face then cascaded over her shoulders. Rock wondered if the curls were as dark beneath the tiny white panties she wore. But the night shadows hid that secret from him.

She wasn't tall, yet she had the longest, shapeliest legs he'd seen in a while. There was nothing in this world he wanted more than to feel them locked around his waist while she moved that ultra-feminine body against his in the heat of passion. He groaned at the image and quickly moved his gaze to her face. It was small and heart-shaped, framed by those wild curls. Her eyes, even in the dark, were big, round and innocent. Rock swallowed hard and looked away from the concern he saw there. The way he felt, he'd probably scare the innocence right out of her.

Unfortunately, his eyes fell to her rather large, full breasts, which sat firm and enticing beneath the snug white T-shirt she wore.

Another mournful growl filled the area around them. He was shocked to realize it was coming from him. Damned if his body didn't choose that moment to show him in full force that it registered just exactly how sexy she was.

Rock attempted to sit up, but a wave of nausea washed over him. As he fought the pain her knee had caused to his groin, he vaguely heard her gasps as she slipped into her jeans.

Rock got to his knees and again attempted to rise. This little vixen really packed a punch. Sweat beaded his brow as he flopped to the ground with a desperate gasp. He was going to cough his cookies, and he didn't want the lady around when he did. "Look, go get me a drink of cold water, will ya?" he growled.

Callie warily regarded the big mountain of a man as he struggled. She'd never hurt anyone before, and the thought that she had injured a perfect stranger in such an intimate way made her feel sick. She prayed that he would be understanding when he was feeling better.

Hesitating for a moment, Callie started up the incline they'd rolled down, but stopped as she heard a choking sound behind her. "Are you going to be okay?"

She was greeted by a wild growl and the sound of the cowboy disgracing himself. She turned and raced to the camper. *Oh, my God, I've probably ruined him for life. How could I have been so clumsy? Lord, what'll I do now?*

Callie dampened a towel and grabbed a bottle of water from her tiny fridge, then raced down the hill to where he lay sprawled on his back, totally still. "Are you all right?" she asked nervously.

"Yeah." He raised a hand to prevent her from coming any closer. "Stay where you are. You are one dangerous lady."

Ignoring his order and his observation, she knelt beside him and placed the shockingly cold towel on his forehead. He pulled it away angrily. "It's not my bloody head that's hurt, it's my—"

"I know what it is," Callie interrupted. "I couldn't very well wrap a cold wet towel around your— Oh, never mind. Here's your water. Do you feel any better now that you've...you know, emptied your stomach?"

He guzzled the water straight from the bottle then swiped at his mouth with the back of his hand. "I'll be just fine, as long as you stay away from me. Look, the reason I stopped was to tell you that your trailer is too close to that curve. I almost rear-ended you. You'd better move it up about twenty feet or so. If you weren't too cheap to pay for a campsite, none of this would have happened."

Callie bristled like a porcupine as she rose to her feet, the wet towel in one hand, the bottle of water in the other. "Now, look here, mister! Just because you've had a little accident and got hurt—through no fault of mine, I might add—doesn't mean you can be condescending with me."

Rock shakily rose to his knees then his feet. Sucking in several deep breaths, he shook his head. "I am not being condescending, lady. And what do you mean, through no fault of yours? I wasn't the one who came barreling out of that door like a cannonball out of hell. I haven't been tackled like that since I was in high school playing football with a bunch of frustrated teenagers. It was plainly one hundred percent your fault." He glared at her.

Callie swore under her breath. "It was not. Any man with any sense would have protected himself during a fall like that, and besides, you shouldn't be knocking on doors at this hour of the night. I might have had a shotgun to protect myself."

"Sweet Jesus and all saints, you'd have killed us both." He glanced toward the heavens for a brief second. "How the hell, pray tell, was I to know what was coming when you opened that door? You city women are all the same, all spit and fire and no sense. Why, you don't even have the common courtesy to take blame and apologize when it's clearly your fault. I'm not standing around for any more of this garbage. Just move the camper before you get yourself killed." Rock climbed the incline as quickly as his injury allowed and reached his truck just as she appeared at the top of the small ridge. "And if I were you, lady, I'd tie a bell around my neck, just to warn people that danger lurks nearby."

2

ROCK WAS LOOKING a bit peaked the next morning when he joined his brothers at the table for breakfast.

"What's wrong with you? You look like you got kicked in the groin. Bad luck at the rodeo yesterday?" Roarke asked.

Rock swallowed at the memory of what had happened, not that he'd had an opportunity to forget it. He may as well have brought her home with him last night for the amount of rest he'd received.

When he'd finally found some sleep, she was there in his dreams, standing over him in her little white lace panties holding a big whip. He'd been so hot to find out just what was under those panties. But whenever he got close and swallowed a breath of her special scent, a big cricket jumped between them and knocked him down the hill.

The dream had repeated itself until he'd woken hard as a rock and frustrated beyond anything he'd experienced in years.

She was one of the most stubborn, spitfire women he'd ever met, and he sincerely hoped he never set eyes on her again.

Roarke cleared his throat, and Rock found himself the object of his brothers' jovial speculation.

"You're looking a little green around the gills,

brother, but I don't smell any booze on you." Reese let the observation hang in the air.

Rock cleared his throat. "Had a little run-in up on Mitchell's Curve." He explained what had happened, waving his hand and dismissing it as inconsequential. His brothers winced. They had both suffered similar damage at some time in their lives, but never at the hands of a woman.

"You gonna be all right?" Roarke asked as he bit into his burned toast.

"I'll survive." Rock swallowed hard and waited to see if his breakfast was going to stay down.

Roarke wisely changed the subject. "I wonder what happened to the architect Alex Master's was sending? He was supposed to be here yesterday."

"Search me. I suppose one of us should stick around to show him where to park. Didn't Alex mention he was bringing a trailer?" Reese stated between bites of his breakfast. He smirked to himself as Rock pushed away his plate looking more than a little unsettled.

Roarke glanced at Rock. "What about you? Do you want to take it easy around the house and wait for him, or shall I?"

"You do it. I don't feel much like being social today. I think I'll check those cattle out in the north hills." Rock slowly rose. A wave of nausea washed over him, and he hesitated until it passed.

Damn that little jinx! It was bad enough she had knocked him off his feet last night and that he'd suffered the worst night since he'd discovered girls, but was there no mercy? Had he not suffered enough?

Ignoring his brothers' speculative stares, he filled his canteen with coffee, grabbed a bag of his favorite cookies and headed toward the barn. What he needed most this morning was peace and quiet, the kind he got out in the wide-open spaces of the ranch. After last night he needed time to think and straighten out his head.

THE ARCHED SIGN said Blue Sky Ranch. Callie gazed at the twenty-foot, hand-carved sign that stretched across the tree-lined lane. It was old and sturdy, like she expected the ranch would be. Fresh spring air billowed into the truck as she rolled down the window. She drew in a deep breath and sighed, contentment seeping into her in spite of the fact she'd still been hopping mad two minutes ago.

If it hadn't been for a park ranger coming to her rescue early this morning, she might still be out there on the top of that mountain waiting for help. He was well equipped to deal with emergencies such as Callie's. He'd helped her fix the tire with a product that temporarily sealed the leak, poured some gas into the tank, then he'd followed her down the mountain to the nearest filling station.

The ranger had known of Blue Sky and the McCall brothers. He'd given her good directions and she'd only been on the road for a half hour before she came across the sign.

At long last she had arrived. Somehow, now that she was here, it didn't seem so bad.

At least she wouldn't have to tow this hunk of junk around any longer. She had no intention of hauling it with her when she left. If her brother wanted the darned thing, he could come and get it himself.

Callie drove over the cattle guard and bumped down the hard-packed dirt lane. Winter frosts had created deep potholes and raised crevasses that spring hadn't gotten around to smoothing out yet. But the fresh air made up for the uncomfortable ride and the bone-jarring bumps.

Rounding a surprisingly smooth curve, Callie gasped at the sight before her eyes. She stopped and stared. Nestled in a shallow valley was a small but beautiful turquoise lake. Tall pines grew around it and into the hill beyond. Large black cattle grazed on the lush green grass.

Callie felt a long-forgotten calmness together with a flutter of excitement. This was beautiful and an absolutely ideal setting for a Masters log home. She drank in the view and smiled. This might turn out to be a job she'd enjoy, after all.

She began to look forward to meeting these people who had the common sense to see that the only choice for a house in this setting was one made of logs.

ROARKE AMBLED out of the house toward the old Jeep and its rickety trailer. Something nudged at the edge of his memory, but he couldn't quite place it. He soon forgot his thoughts when a small, shapely young woman with a mane of black curls slipped from the vehicle and bounced over to him.

Removing her dark glasses, she looked at him with a hundred-watt smile and presented her hand. "Hi, I'm Callie Masters. Alex sent me." Her smile suddenly brightened. "You're Roarke McCall. I'd forgot-ten—I hadn't put the name with the face until this very moment. I'm glad to be here."

Roarke remembered her as a child. It had been years since he'd seen Alex's little sister.

When he and Alex had been in college together, Roarke had often gone home with Alex on weekends. In no time he'd become like the third Masters son. Seeing Callie brought those comfortable memories back.

She also brought back memories of a beautiful child who had teased and flirted with him when he was a kid away from home for the first time. He'd predicted then that she would grow to be a beauty, and she had.

Throughout the years since Roarke and Alex had graduated they had stayed in touch, and Alex had told him of Callie's extensive training in engineering and architecture. He had also explained about the failed wedding and the resulting change in Callie. But Roarke would have never guessed who she was if she hadn't introduced herself. Never had Alex men-tioned how beautiful his young sister had become.

Clearing his throat, Roarke took her hand with a welcoming smile. "How are you, Callie? I haven't seen you since you were nine or ten years old. You've sure grown into a beautiful woman. I'm looking for-ward to getting to know you all over again." He paused, thinking she might take that the wrong way. "Alex has bragged so much about your accomplish-ments, I'm wondering how we rate the best of the firm."

"Well, I wouldn't let Alex hear you say that," she stated confidently with a smile that could knock a man right off his feet. "But it's a busy time of year, and I guess they figured I needed the break from the big city."

She glanced around, avoiding Roarke's eyes. She knew the hurt was still there for anyone to see, and she didn't want to talk about it.

"You have a beautiful tract of land here, Roarke. I'm happy you decided to go with a log construction. This is the perfect place for the natural beauty of a wood home."

Roarke gazed at her, surprised at the surge of brotherly protection that suddenly nudged him. "I'm glad you think so, Callie. I take it Alex told you that if my brothers like your ideas they'll want you to plan and build for them, too?"

"Yes, he mentioned it, but they aren't sure, are they?" She flashed a dimpled smile at him. "I can take care of that. I'll be glad to stay on as long as there's a need. This is a beautiful spot. I'm going to enjoy my stay." She sighed as she scanned the area. "Now if you'll just tell me where I can park my home, we can get started." Callie wanted to settle in fast. She was anxious to investigate the area that would be her home for the summer.

"You can park next to the drive shed. There are electrical and water hookups over there. Plus you'll have the protection of the shed if a storm blows up. There's a washroom in the office in the shed. Feel free to use both of them. None of us use them anymore."

Callie smiled, nodded and turned to get into her truck, but Roarke's voice stopped her.

"I'd like you to come to the house for supper tonight and meet my brothers. You could bring some of your plans with you and we can have a quick peek at what you're doing these days." Roarke winked at her, and Callie was momentarily transported to her childhood.

"Thank you, Roarke. I'll be there, plans in hand. I think I'm going to enjoy this job." She smiled as she climbed into her Jeep.

Roarke stood watching her with something niggling at his memory. Suddenly things started adding up. Was this the camper Rock had met last evening? A smirk began on Roarke's face. This was going to be some summer.

What he remembered of Callie at ten was sheer tomboy devilry. She could give as well as she got. Put her with that cocky youngest brother of his and presto, instant dynamite and a battle of wills. If anyone could give Rock a run for his money, it was this little spitfire.

He watched her park the trailer with the ease of a seasoned transport driver and turned away with a chuckle. He was going to enjoy this.

If it wasn't for the sneaky suspicion that all hell was about to break loose, Roarke might have prepared his brothers for their guest. Instead he sat tight and said little. There were bound to be fireworks once Callie left, but he hoped she'd have proven her architectural ability to them by then. On the other hand, knowing Rock, the fireworks might not wait until she left.

Then again, if Callie Masters was anything like what he remembered, she might be the one to explode first.

His curiosity was piqued. There was no doubt in his mind she'd be able to handle a hardheaded chauvinist like Rock with ease. He just hoped Rock was feeling up to it. After a day in the saddle, chances were he'd be grumpier than an old she bear with a sore paw at mating season.

Well, too bad, Roarke thought with a self-satisfied smirk. They hadn't had a good show around here in ages, and he was positive that Callie could win any fight that came in her direction.

There was something about the sparkle of devilment in Callie's eyes that made him think of his mother. And she had, without a doubt, ruled the roost. Even his big, tough, no-nonsense father had been at her mercy. Just as Roarke suspected they all would be around Callie. He chuckled at the upcoming evening.

"What's so funny?" Reese asked as he flopped onto his chair. He filled a huge glass with water and guzzled it down before filling it again. He looked at Roarke, puzzled. "Staying around the house got you a little loco?" Reese stole a biscuit and busied himself buttering it.

Roarke chuckled again. "No, just thinking about the entertainment we're going to be having this evening."

Reese raised his head. "What entertainment?"

"Wait and see. Our architect arrived, and Rock just

may have a fit when he meets Cal." Roarke pulled the roast from the oven as he spoke.

Reese frowned and shook his head. He cast a glance toward his brother, wondering what had happened to Roarke's common sense. "What's going on?" he asked between the two bites that finished the fluffy biscuit.

Roarke held up his hand, "Shh. Here she comes."

CALLIE KNOCKED politely at the faded and warped screen door and waited. They definitely needed a new home. It looked as if a good strong wind could do the demolition job on this place with relative ease. She wondered how it had stood up against Mother Nature this long.

Roarke appeared behind the tattered screen with a welcoming smile. "Callie, come in, dinner's almost ready."

He escorted her into the shabbiest kitchen she'd ever seen in her entire twenty-eight years on this earth. "Have a seat. This here's my brother Reese. Reese, this is Callie, Cal Masters, the architect. Let me take your briefcase, Callie."

Reese was surprised, but his good manners prevented him from showing it. "Cal or Callie? Which do you prefer?" He rose to his feet, tossing a glance at Roarke. It settled into a knowing grin. He held her chair out.

"Most people call me Callie, but I'll answer to almost anything. Anything but honey or lady. It's nice to meet you, Reese. I was saying to your brother earlier that you have the perfect setting here for a log home. I know I'm going to enjoy this project, even if I had some bad luck getting here."

Reese met Roarke's eyes over Callie's shoulder, not missing the look of pure glee that filled his older brother's face. "Bad luck? Did you have trouble finding us?" he inquired, concern in his voice.

"No, not that, but the whole trip was one disaster after another. I started out at six yesterday morning." Callie began to tell of her plight. Just as she got to the part about some twit pounding at her door, the devil himself walked in, dragging his tired old body.

"You!" Callie jumped to her feet with the speed of a bushfire, anger flaring in her eyes. Having just recalled the events of her trip, her temper had edged its way to the surface again. "What are you doing here?"

Rock took one look at the petite dynamo standing in the middle of the kitchen and let out a soulful groan. "Oh, Lord! I've died and gone to hell." He shut his eyes tightly and prayed it was all a nightmare. She'd be gone when he opened them again. But she was still there, in all her living glory.

He was filled with disbelief, then disgust. His body tensed at meeting her when she'd barely been off his mind all day. This was all he needed after the day he'd put in. Did the gods have no mercy whatsoever? "What the hell are *you* doing here?"

"Rock!" Reese and Roarke both admonished him for his manners.

Callie was so incensed at finding the culprit of her nightmares or—heaven forbid—fantasies here in this peaceful haven that she didn't notice that the two McCall men obviously knew the scallywag.

"What I'm doing here isn't the question, buster, it's what you're doing here that's important. Did you follow me here? Are you looking for a little retribution for your clumsiness last night?" Callie bristled, but stood up to him like David to Goliath.

Roarke and Reese both backed off to watch the fireworks. It became clear to them that Callie was indeed the she devil Rock had his little run-in with late last night. Already sparks were flying, just as Roarke had somehow known they would.

"What am *I* doing here?" Rock tossed his hat and canteen on the crowded sofa just inside the door. "Lady, I live here. This is my home. Now, would you tell me what the hell *you're* doing here?" Rock leaned against the counter, crossing his long, heavily muscled legs. That action hurt like the devil. He folded his arms over his chest and he waited in quiet agony as she came up with an answer.

"I happen to be the architect Mr. McCall has hired to build his new home." Callie didn't look as confident as she sounded.

Rock glanced at Roarke for confirmation and groaned. A lady architect. A lady trying to do a man's job. Lord, sweet Lord. What had Roarke gotten them into? He approached Callie and stood towering over her. He liked the fact that she had to look way up to face him.

"It's obvious you've managed to pull the wool over somebody's eyes. But we don't have time to pussyfoot around out here in the country. We work hard and expect to see results quickly. I thought Alex Masters had more sense than to be swayed by a pair of dark eyes and a knockout body."

Roarke froze. Until now he'd been setting food on the table and enjoying the sight of this little lady sparring with his overconfident younger brother. He'd just decided to step in before things got downright dirty, but before he had the chance, Callie answered Rock.

She edged closer until Rock stepped back. "I'll have you know, you arrogant stuffed shirt, that I have a degree in engineering as well as my architect's license. I've worked hard to get where I am today. In fact, I've had to work harder than most of those so-called men who supposedly have brains in their heads. I've often had to correct their mistakes. I'm probably going to have to correct many more stupid male mistakes. In fact, last night proved it as plain as daylight."

Callie stepped back, her arms crossed over her shapely breasts and her legs braced in a wide stance, waiting for his counterattack.

Fiery blue eyes burned into him, and her cheeks flushed brightly. And topping it off was that mane of wild black curls. He'd never forget the stunning picture she made as long as he lived. She was life at its fullest, its best. She was anger personified. Not that her anger stopped Rock. He was so wrapped up in his side of the fight that he couldn't have seen a train coming toward him at full speed.

"Why, you little vixen," he said menacingly. "You know damn well that was all your fault. The way you came barreling out of that wreck you call a camper, there was no way in hell I could have prevented what happened. I sure hope you have more sense in the world of architectural design than you do choosing a camping spot or we're in bigger trouble than I imagined."

Callie gritted her teeth and clenched her fists. For the first time in her life she really, honestly wanted to resort to violence. But a lady didn't do that sort of thing to a man who wasn't her brother, especially when that man was a prospective customer. But it was tempting, so very tempting.

"You overgrown baboon, if you'd opened your eyes last night you would have realized I had a flat tire on that so-called piece of junk that is my home for the summer. Why the devil would I have parked it there if I'd had a choice? Especially since I was so close to my goal. I had to wait until this morning for a ranger to come along to help. Besides that, you should have had more sense than to pound on a person's door in the middle of the night. What if I'd had a gun?"

"Heaven forbid. It's a damn bell you need around your neck." Rock demonstrated with his hands, but touching her smooth white neck with its rapid pulse throbbing against his thumb set off some cataclysmic chemical reaction that ripped through his body, stunning him.

He pulled his hands away in shock. A quick glance at the woman told him she felt the same way he did. Oh, Lord, trouble. This vixen was going to be trouble.

There was silence—total, electrifying silence—in the room.

Callie was suddenly mortified at the scene the two of them had made and immediately tried to smooth things over. She glanced at Reese and Roarke. "Ah, I guess you figured out that we've already met. Although not on the best of terms."

She turned to Rock, avoiding any contact with his eyes. She presented her hand. "I'm sorry. Callie Masters, Alex's sister, chief designer of Masters Log Homes. I'm sorry about last night. It...it was an accident." She apologized, to be courteous to a customer, although she didn't mean a word of it.

Rock had no choice but to accept her apology. He took her hand and spoke in a quiet, subdued tone, wishing he didn't have to do this. It went against his grain to have to accept her apology. But he had been brought up with manners and was expected to use them. The last thing he needed was to have his brothers ganging up on him. Since she had apologized, he had to accept graciously, although it damned near killed him.

"Rock. My name is Rockwell McCall, and your apology is accepted." He let go of her soft, magnetic hand and glanced at his brothers, who wore knowing, amused, grins.

"Now, if you'll all excuse me I think I'll go upstairs and sit in the tub. Don't wait supper for me. I may be awhile." Rock tilted his hat toward Callie and limped from the room with what pride he had left.

Callie watched him limp away, slightly bowlegged. She hadn't noticed how good-looking he was last night in the dark. Not that she wanted to now. It had been hard enough to keep her mind on the argument with his big brawny chest practically in her face. The same chest she had buried her nose in last night.

He wasn't all that much like his brothers. Oh, he had the dark hair and the tall, rough stance of the other McCalls. But he was leaner and younger than the other two, taller and more muscular. He had a devil-may-care look about him. His shoulders were wide, he had legs like tree trunks, and he possessed the tiniest little hips and a tight rounded butt.

Wild streaks of red slashed through his dark hair, which made her think he probably was the same in personality. That same red imitated itself in his mustache, a bushy one that covered his entire upper lip.

Callie had never been kissed by a man with a mustache, and she wondered for a second what it would be like. Her active imagination carried that thought one step further and she wondered what a mustache would feel like brushing over her body. She immediately put a stop to that train of thought and turned her attention to the other two men.

"Well." Roarke blurted out into the stillness. "Supper is ready and on the table. You'll have to excuse Rock, Callie. He isn't normally so quick-tempered. It's just after last night he's a little...ah..." Callie watched as the big man before her turned a dull red.

"Tender," Reese said. "Sit down, Callie. Have some supper and tell us about your designs." Reese easily defused the situation with his gracious personality and warm smile.

Callie considered the doorway Rock had disappeared through and sighed quietly. She really did feel bad about what had happened last night and about

the argument tonight. Things seemed to get out of
hand so easily when she came face-to-face with him.
It was as if there was some off-center attraction or
something at work between them. But that couldn't
be. She wouldn't let it.

ROCK SLOWLY EASED his bulk down into the barely
warm water that filled the old claw-foot tub. He
winced. How could a small-boned female create such
havoc in his body? He wouldn't have believed it if he
hadn't been the bearer of the swollen, bruised area
between his thighs.

It didn't help that for a minute, down there in the
kitchen, he'd felt the unmistakable swelling of
arousal bear down on him. That was what had made
him give up on the battle and stop the arguing he was
so enjoying.

Rock shook his head. She was pure fire. A spitfire,
his father would have labeled her. He found himself
smiling. He'd never met a woman like her before. She
was small, but she harbored an energy that was difficult to resist. She had such a hot temper and was so
determined. When she'd stood her ground, a man
barely had a chance. If she didn't get you by that
quick tongue, then her sexy little body would do the
job.

Closing his eyes, he recalled the way her eyes had
burned as blue as sapphires on a sunny day. And
those dimples, oh, Lord, those dimples. They had in-
grained themselves even deeper into his mind than
her smooth, flushed cheeks. She had been magnificent in her anger and shockingly feminine in her

apology. Never had he met such a mixture of personalities and contradictions in one small package.

For the first time in his life, he'd met a woman who could stand up to him. As infuriating as she was, he had to admit, he liked that. She'd probably be like fire in his bed. And under different circumstances he might have tried to get her there. But all she signified to him at the moment was pain and agonizing temptation.

As he sank into the water, he cursed, disgusted as he looked at the hardening power of his sex. "Get down, you stupid twit, you're in no condition to even think about that, let alone try it. What are you trying to do, kill me? Damn, she's got me talking to my body parts now." Rock threw up his hands. "She's a witch." A beautiful, sexy witch with black silky hair and never-ending legs who packed one hell of a punch.

He forced himself to relax and drifted off to sleep, half immersed in the cool water, half immersed in a fantasy dream with one black-haired witch dressed in white lace panties that left little to the imagination. She made his heart pound like never before and his blood throb. And then there was the grasshopper....

LATE THAT NIGHT, after an encouraging evening with Reese and Roarke, Callie headed to her camper. She had spent some time in the big drive shed office this afternoon, cleaning out the shower and setting up her drafting equipment. Now she intended to make full use of the shower.

She needed something to help soothe and relax her

or she'd never sleep. The disagreement and her un-expected feelings for Rock McCall left her slightly off-kilter. The thought that she had done some per-manent damage to him upset her greatly.

He had looked pretty uncomfortable when he had left the kitchen, and he hadn't reappeared all eve-ning. However, they *had* heard him shuffling around upstairs when they had cleared the table to look over some of the plans she'd brought along.

She stripped out of her clothes, adjusted the tem-perature and stepped into the shower. The last thing she needed was to distract herself with a chauvinistic cowboy who didn't even have enough sense in his bull head to look after himself. He shouldn't have been so stubborn as to go out on horseback after his accident. Even *she* knew that.

Callie tried to push him out of her mind. He was an overconfident, macho smart aleck with big muscular arms and broad shoulders. He probably had one of those washboard stomachs to go along with his nar-row hips and strong, muscular thighs. And he prob-ably knew how to use those hips to pleasure a woman just the way she liked it, too. She could hang on to those big broad shoulders and enjoy riding a man like... *What the devil am I thinking?* Callie twisted off the hot stream of water and grabbed her towel, dis-gusted with herself.

"I will not think about Rock McCall. I will not get involved. I will *not* get involved. I do not want to get involved with him." She dried herself off and shrugged into her favorite oversize terry robe.

She hadn't expected to have this problem because she hadn't thought to find any interesting men here.

Callie was truthful enough with herself to admit that Rock McCall was good-looking, but she was also sure she could ignore the attraction she felt.

After all, he was only a man. And she'd really had it with men. She'd been so stupid to believe that Peter was everything that she wanted in a man. He had pushed and shoved her around, making her change her beliefs and goals to suit his. And she'd let him. He'd flattered her and she'd convinced herself that what he offered was what she wanted.

Then it had all blown up in her face. She'd learned that you had to trust those inner feelings or you end up betraying yourself, and that was the worst crime to commit. She'd learned her lesson well. Tall, handsome men made a lifetime hobby of assuring themselves they were still good-looking. A woman didn't have a chance with a good-looker. She was committing herself to waiting for him to find someone who made him feel more handsome.

Callie didn't have the time or energy to stroke an oversize ego. She wanted a simple life, a life with a man with whom she shared mutual love and respect. Not a man like Rock McCall, not at all.

She did a fine job of convincing herself of that until she drifted off to sleep. He was in her dreams, waiting for her, flat on his back dressed in only a smile.

Shortly after midnight Callie woke to the sound of a car arriving in the yard. She looked out the window and watched as a stooped older man made his way into the well-lit house carrying a black bag. The doctor, Callie realized, her thoughts swinging immediately to Rock. He really hadn't looked well earlier.

The doctor stayed for over an hour. Apparently Rock was in great discomfort and pain. As much as Callie hated to admit it, some of it *was* her fault.

She flopped into the narrow bed and sighed regretfully. What a way to start off a working relationship—any kind of a relationship, for that matter.

IT WAS TWO DAYS before Callie got another glimpse of Rock. Endless days wherein she kept busy staking out the area Roarke had chosen for his new home and working on the revisions he wanted to the plan he'd chosen—anything to keep her mind off the man in the big farmhouse.

Rumor from the various ranch hands she'd met verified that the doctor had indeed come for Rock, although nobody would let on just what was wrong with him. Everyone just chuckled and joked in a roundabout way. Everyone but her.

Callie had no doubt that Rock's condition was serious, and she felt sick at the thought that she might have had something to do with his suffering. When she finally caught a glimpse of him in the flesh, she felt a hundred percent better. So much better, in fact, that when she saw him ease himself down onto the porch swing, she gathered her courage to walk over and talk with him awhile.

"Hi, it's good to see you up and around," she greeted him cheerfully. "How are you feeling?"

Rock looked at her with caution in his eyes. She looked just as she had in his many fever-induced dreams over the past couple of days—and just as dangerous. It made him furious. He put his hand straight out to stop her from approaching. "Don't come any closer. I can't risk it. You have no idea what I've been through."

"I'm sorry," Callie murmured, taken aback by the implication that she was totally responsible. It hurt her deeply that he still blamed her for the entire fiasco. She studied him from eight feet away. He looked washed out, as if he'd been deathly ill. His eyes drooped and his face was pale. She had no doubt he'd had a rough few days.

"Will you be...I mean is the damage, um..." She chewed on her bottom lip as she shifted from one foot to the other.

Rock watched with a tingle of delicious malice. She struggled with her embarrassment. He gave her no lead, letting her fumble for the words.

It wasn't that he was mean or spiteful, it was just that he was kind of lonely and fed up with his own company. Since the doctor had demanded that he not go near a horse or any other work for at least a week, he was desperate for conversation. Not that he would come right out and ask her. That would be admitting that he was interested, and he couldn't have her thinking that.

Anyway, it was fascinating to watch the different colors her face became and the way she was scuffling in the dirt to avoid meeting his eyes.

Callie tried again. "What I'm trying to say is..." She blushed beet red. Rock wondered if she might be an innocent. "Are you going to be sterile from the damage?" she blurted.

Rock chuckled, suddenly feeling sorry he'd put her through it all. He forgot his hesitation, she looked so worried. He couldn't let her feel any more guilt over the situation. "No, I'm not going to be sterile. I wrenched a muscle getting off my horse, and the swelling from the knock I took didn't help matters. But to be honest, it was a bout of flu that put me down. I'm fine now, just a little achy and weak. I hate that more than anything." He paused and his voice gentled. "Look, I'm sorry if you thought it was all your fault. It wasn't. Come up and talk with me a bit. Tell me about your work. Roarke has been raving over the design he's chosen and your revisions." He patted the empty space beside him on the swing.

Callie hesitated, angry because he'd let her embarrass herself worrying about his private parts when there was really nothing to worry about. That was her own fault, she supposed. Nobody had said what it was he was suffering with. She'd jumped to conclusions.

She approached cautiously. The last thing she needed was some stupid accident to happen. She stood by the railing and talked to him about the weather and how wonderful she thought the area was. He told her of some local attractions she'd have to visit before she headed home and suggested that an overnight trip might be enjoyable. They bantered back and forth until they were both relaxed.

When Rock suggested a cold drink, Callie popped into the kitchen. At her return she was feeling so much more comfortable. She handed Rock his glass of lemonade and plopped down beside him on the old porch swing. Unfortunately, she kept on going down, down, down, until they both landed with a loud crash and a hard thump, followed by a long, low groan that turned into a growl.

3

CALLIE LAY FROZEN, watching the lemonade slosh in the glass she still held upright in her hand. Not a drip spilled.

She glanced hesitantly over to the cowboy who lay awkwardly amongst the broken pieces of the porch swing. One very long and loud groan of agony came from him, followed by another.

Callie winced. This had to be some kind of weird coincidence or something. Twice now she'd knocked this guy off his feet.

The humor in the situation struck her at that moment. Biting her lip, trying her best to contain the laughter that was bubbling in her throat, she almost choked. The stupidity of it all was simply overwhelming. The dam burst, and her laughter filled the air around them.

The giant on the floor beside her growled something unintelligible.

"This is not my fault." Callie managed to speak through the tears of amusement that streamed down her face. The situation was so ridiculous she couldn't help it. No matter how hard she tried to control her laughter, she couldn't stop.

Rock attempted to ignore her. He hadn't even caught what was left of his breath and she was howling with laughter. He groaned, more in disgust than agony. What was it with this woman?

If this vixen was out to kill him, she was doing a good job of it, slowly but surely, bit by bit, prolonging the inevitable death as long as she could. He was like a worm on a hook, and she was having great fun dangling him before she did him in.

As if he hadn't suffered enough over the past few days. He was paying for his sins, and he didn't like it one bit. Lying in his sickbed he'd prayed for forgiveness for all the times he had teased his brothers unmercifully when they had been down and out.

He'd also discovered a few things about himself and his bed that he didn't like. First and most distressing was the fact that he had a complete intolerance for pain. Second was that he slept in the most uncomfortable bed in the world. Not only was it too short, but it was lumpy.

And then there was his vivid and very active imagination. When he had nothing to keep his mind and body busy, he was prone to fantasies about his tormentor that tested his body right to the limit.

In his hours of discomfort he had vowed to be a nicer person to everyone, including this jinx. But all good intentions seemed to have disappeared as he lay listening to her yukking it up at his expense.

"Shut up. Just shut up. Can't you see I'm hurt here?" In a voice filled with fury and distress, he cursed and told her in choice words what he thought of her laughter. He ended his tirade abruptly as something very sharp snagged his pants and jabbed the tender skin of his butt.

Callie floundered in the face of his anger. "Oh, come on McCall. Surely you can see the humor in the situation." Awkwardly, she scrambled to her feet.

"Anybody ever mention the word jinx in the same sentence as your name?" he asked sarcastically. She shook her head cautiously. "Well, I am!"

Gnawing on her bottom lip, Callie surveyed Rock's awkward position. Boy, talk about déjà vu. Hadn't she seen him in a similar position mere days ago? How the devil had this happened? And why now, when they were beginning to get along?

"Are you all right?" Callie asked in a subdued voice. "Give me your hand and I'll pull you up."

"Forget it. Get lost, Jinx," Rock growled. "Go away before you end up killing me." He attempted to shift his weight, but couldn't. A moan in pure frustration slipped from his tightly clamped lips. "Sweet Jesus and all saints," he swore between clenched teeth as he reached beneath his body to dislodge a piece of broken and splintered wood.

Not only had he pulled a muscle, he'd gotten himself trapped here by a sharp object that held his butt to the ground. "Go find someone to help me. Someone very big and very strong. And don't you dare come back. Stay away from me!"

Callie hesitated before she took off running to the nearest barn. As much as she would have loved to stay and argue with him, she thought better of it. It appeared that he was in pain. And the fact that she could hear his curses and groans across the barnyard did not sit well with her conscience.

In her mind's eye she could see Rock sprawled on

top of the fallen porch swing. The panicky pounding of her heart carried a genuine stab of regret and despair.

Maybe some wicked and spiteful witch had placed a spell on her, or maybe God was out to get her. Whoever, they were doing a darn good job.

ROARKE AND REESE were rolling with laughter when Callie finally ventured over to the house to ask about Rock. The doctor had been in again that afternoon. She'd heard the angry curses through Rock's open bedroom window for a good half hour as the man had attended to him.

Callie approached the two men, who sat on the top step of the porch, enjoying the warm evening and a cool beer. "Ah, hi."

"Hey, Callie," Reese greeted her. "I guess you're feeling pretty sore this evening, too. You sure you're okay? You didn't do any damage this afternoon, did you?"

"No, I'm fine. How is Rock?" she asked boldly, still stinging from Rock's sharp words when Roarke and another hand had pulled him from the wreckage of the swing. Her face flared into a hot blush at the memory. "I heard him earlier, when the doctor was here. Is he all right?"

"He's fine, Callie, and no matter what he says, it was not your fault. This house is so old that everything is falling apart. That porch swing has been a hazard for years. Rock should have known better." Roarke spoke firmly. He took a long guzzle from the bottle held loosely in his hand, then very smoothly changed the subject. "Now, how are the plans coming?"

Callie had been working on the revisions to his house while they waited for the arrival of a crew to clear a spot for the foundation.

"I'm almost finished, should be done tomorrow. This little incident kind of threw me off today." She wrinkled her nose and pulled at the narrow hem of her denim shorts.

"There's no rush, Callie. Take all the time you need. And don't concern yourself with Rock. He's fine, really."

"Then why was he cursing when the doctor was here?" Callie raised her chin as if demanding that Roarke not hide the seriousness of the accident from her.

Reese chuckled and Roarke tried to keep a straight face while he explained the delicate state Rock was in. "Ah, he had some slivers, ah, and the doctor was removing them. I think you can guess where they were."

Callie winced.

"Now, he can't ride for a week. Can't really sit down, either. It's kind of good to see him finally getting a taste of how uncomfortable life can be. Until you came on the scene, Callie, he'd kind of floated through life never having an accident and never being too sympathetic to those of us who did. Now he's getting his share, and I'm enjoying the hell out of it." Reese snickered.

Men were strange in the way they reasoned things out. She wondered how Reese could be so callous.

Rock had to be very uncomfortable, and all his brother could do was joke about it.

When Roarke joined in the laughter, Callie shook her head and looked heavenward. *Men.* She thought she saw a movement at Rock's bedroom window. But there was no one there. Rock was probably asleep. Surely the doctor had given him pain medication. That thought made her feel somewhat better.

"Want a beer, Callie?"

"Uh, pardon? I'm sorry, my mind was wandering." She glanced at Reese, who stood by the door waiting for an answer.

"A beer. Would you like one?" he asked again, his eyebrows raised.

"Ah, no, I think I'll turn in early. Thanks, anyway." She said her good-nights and slowly made her way to the trailer, knowing she was being watched by more than one set of McCall eyes.

Once she reached the dark shadows of the trailer, Callie glanced toward the window again. Rock stood there, silhouetted by the light behind him. He wore nothing but a stark white towel around his hips. The towel contrasted sharply with his deep tan. His chest was covered in a thick mat of hair, and in his hand was a bottle of beer.

He was staring right at her.

If Callie had had any doubt that he could see her, she would have hidden. Instead she sat in silent appreciation, watching him.

Lord, but he was a beautiful example of virility. She watched as he lifted the bottle to his lips and drained it. Giving her a jaunty little salute and a nod, he turned away and let the towel drop. Callie gasped. Even from this distance she could see his well-muscled backside before he doused his bedroom light and disappeared into the darkness.

Callie sat for a long while thinking, wishing that she'd never laid eyes on the cowboy, but admitting that she'd have missed an eyeful if she had. In town he would have been considered a prime male. In her mind he was nothing but trouble and potential heartache. She had to remember that men brought pain and upset.

She'd worked hard to get ahead in the fancy uptown firm of architects where she'd met her fiancé. She'd produced some startling and prize-winning building designs only to have Peter take credit for them. But she'd loved him, so she'd let it go. Then his parents had decided that Callie was below their station in life, so they'd bribed Peter. If he broke off the engagement, they would buy the firm.

Peter hadn't hesitated, grabbing at the glory of having his own business. He'd dumped Callie without a second thought, and because of the discomfort between them he'd fired her over a technicality.

After all these months, losing her job hurt more than losing him did. She'd lost her independence and had to go crawling to the family firm. That had killed something inside her.

If she could just get everything into perspective and remember what men were really like, maybe she'd have a chance fighting the attraction she felt for Rock McCall.

THE NIGHT WAS HOT for early June. Callie had been tossing and turning for hours, thinking of Rock. She hadn't seen him much all week.

Frustrated and angry with herself for thinking about him when she'd already given herself so many lectures on the evils of men, she decided to sit outside and have a cold drink rather than to battle insomnia.

She had worked long into the night every day this week hoping to exhaust herself. She'd drawn up the first plans for Reese's house and construction of Roarke's log home was well under way.

The humidity was high, the air close and still. Callie searched the dark sky wondering if they might get a storm. She hadn't listened to the weather report earlier and it was too late now. The only station she could get on her small portable set played nonstop music at night.

She pulled the cotton T-shirt nightie away from her body and waved it a bit, cooling herself. It occurred to her that there were lighter, more comfortable pieces of nightwear she could be dressed in, and she slipped inside to change.

Dressed in a scant pair of tap pants and a light camisole of pink silk, she slipped into the screened area outside the trailer. The breeze had picked up while she was inside, and off in the distance she could hear the first faint rumbles of thunder. Someone else was getting the storm. She could relax.

She sat on the big lounger, enjoying the breeze in the sultry evening. Not surprisingly, sleep took her to where a big, brawny mountain man once again waited for her.

AT THAT MOMENT, Rock was pacing at his bedroom window enjoying the first breeze they'd had all week. The heat had just about driven him crazy, and he swore his new house would be equipped with air-conditioning.

It didn't help much that she—the vixen who was more dangerous than any rabid fox he'd run into—was so close at hand.

He had watched her for days now. Even though he warned himself to stop, he'd find himself at the window waiting for a glimpse of her curved figure or her sensuous, straight-backed walk. He had developed a near obsession with that long, curly black hair, but what man wouldn't fantasize about wrapping himself in it?

He'd watched every morning as she set out on her regular walk. She didn't just stroll. She took long, quick strides, as if she had an urgent purpose.

One afternoon he'd watched her strip down to what he considered a scant one-piece bathing suit that barely held her luscious breasts. As she'd laid in the sun he'd almost rushed down to beat one of the ranch hands for whistling at her.

He'd watched the lights in her trailer reflect her silhouette and thought he'd go insane with the strength of his desire. And he watched with concern as she kept working over the table in the shed office long after midnight.

Tonight he'd watched her in the small room at the back of the trailer. He'd seen her pull off the nightshirt and he'd agonized over her perfect silhouette. Now he was plagued with a different type of aching, a type that only one vixen was going to be able to cure.

Lying down on his bed, he rolled onto his stomach to compress that insistent arousal that had become a constant in his life since she'd shown up a mere two weeks ago. His body seemed to have a mind of its own lately, and it only served to remind him of what he couldn't have.

Tossing, turning and cursing, he began finally to drift toward sleep. His mind wandered until she was beneath him, breathless, urging him along with softly uttered moans and sighs. He was buried in her tight warmth and felt as if he'd come home at last. Relief, blessed relief filled his body.

Rock woke with a start, ready to explode, his pillow squashed beneath him. He cursed none too delicately and willed the cry of his hormones to a dull roar. A blast of thunder shook the house, and Rock bounded out of bed as lightning crackled so close to the house that he could almost see sparks. The rain they'd been praying for seemed to have arrived in a fury.

His first thought was for Callie in that rickety old trailer. He slipped to the window and peered out. Everything seemed to be all right. Neon-bright flashes of lightning allowed him to see that the trailer was still in one piece, although it rocked with the gusts of wind that careened down the mountainside.

He forced himself to lay in his bed and listened as the storm buffeted the house and generally caused havoc outside.

In many ways he loved a storm, but as a rancher

and a farmer, he despised them. He thought of the cows and new calves on the range and of the time he and his brothers had helped put out a barn fire started by lightning. All the animals inside had perished. The farmer had lost everything. His life had been destroyed in one uncontrolled strike.

Mother Nature was a powerful partner, unpredictable and fierce as she was giving and gentle.

Muttering to himself he gave in to his worry over Callie. He slipped on a flannel shirt and jeans and tiptoed down the stairs. It was stupid for her to stay out there and endanger her life. After all, this was no regular storm, and that rig of hers was far from solid.

Why hadn't his brothers thought about that? Surely they'd heard a weather forecast before they went to bed. Why hadn't they had the foresight to bring her inside where she'd at least be safe? He crept into the kitchen, wondering where Roarke had put his boots.

Lightning flashed and lit his way through the darkness.

He was at the back door when he noticed a shadow on the couch in the corner of the kitchen. Approaching quietly, he heard the faint sound of sobbing.

It stunned him.

A bright flash illuminated a small lump huddled on the couch beneath a blanket. It was shaking. It was too small to be either of his brothers. The feminine snuffs were a dead giveaway.

"Callie?" he whispered, then jumped back as if he expected her to strike out at him. She stayed perfectly still and whispered her reply without removing the blanket from her head.

"Go away." Her voice came out as a weak tiny whisper.

"Are you all right?" he asked, then mentally kicked himself. It was obvious to anyone who had ears that she was not.

"I'm fine." The nasally spoken words were followed by a great gasping breath.

"That was pretty convincing. You're not fine at all. Take that silly blanket off your head and talk to me."

"No." She sobbed, then jumped at the next crash of thunder.

"Ah, you're frightened of the storm. I don't blame you. I'm a little more than uncomfortable about it myself. Take the blanket off your head, and we'll have a drink and sit out the storm together," Rock suggested.

"I d-don't think so. Ev-every time I get near you, you end up getting h-hurt. You b-better go back to your bed." She hiccuped and took in another sniffy breath.

Rock gently sat on the edge of the sofa beside her and pulled away the downy soft blanket that he knew was not one of theirs. She was shaking like a leaf beneath it, and her eyes were as big as an owl's. "Now tell me, surely you're not that frightened of storms?"

"What if I am? It's my business," Callie answered miserably, then jumped at the roar of the next bout of thunder. "Yes, I am, I hate it. It's so loud here in the mountains," Callie blurted. "It brings back all the memories and the pain. I hate it." She moved into Rock's waiting arms and clung to his shoulder.

Rock was stunned at her admission and lost at her tears. He'd never had a woman cry on his shoulder before. Heck, he'd never even seen a woman cry before, except Great-Aunt Ettie. Not that it had been anywhere near his shoulder. It was rather frightening as well as unnerving. She nuzzled closer and hiccuped. *What do I do now?* "Are you better?" The question brought on a whole new slew of tears.

"Now look, there's no need for this. Stop crying at once. The storm's not going to hurt you." He tried to shock her out of it with a little force.

"I know." But she sobbed even harder, and he found himself reacting in a totally unexpected way as she curled herself closer to him. He felt a sudden welling up of protectiveness. He was determined that nothing would harm her. His body became shivery and decidedly hard all over. Especially that male part of him that was in acute danger whenever he was near her.

He attempted to push her away, not wanting her to feel his reaction to the scant silky outfit that she was wearing. Nor did he need to feel her nuzzled against his body.

"Look, sweetheart, I'm sorry you're so scared and that the storm has upset you, but I don't know what to do for you," Rock said helplessly, holding on to her but thinking he really ought to let her go.

"You're doing just f-fine." She sniffed. "You're big and strong and I don't have anything to f-fear now."

With that, she sniffed and sighed, and while he was

still searching for something soothing to say, her breathing slowed to an even pace. He held her firmly, and it occurred to him that she had been awfully still for some time. He wondered if she'd gone to sleep.

He looked at her dark wet eyelashes fanning over her pale damp cheeks, and his heart jumped. Yes, she had. She had fallen asleep right in his arms.

Lord, but she did feel good all pressed up against him. Rock closed his eyes and gloried in her warmth. He could easily get used to this feeling.

The thunder rumbled in the distance leaving the rain and wind behind. Rock felt a whole new storm building inside him. He sucked in a deep breath and tried to release the pressure mounting in his chest. His heart trembled as he looked at her.

Right from square one, he'd known she'd be trouble for him. But he was just beginning to realize exactly what kind of trouble she represented. He hadn't expected the emotion and the passion she caused in him. The attraction, yes, but not the emotion.

He'd always managed to keep the ladies at arm's length, not allowing any of them to breach the walls he'd erected around his heart. But if he wasn't careful, this one would slip under the barricade and attack even before he was aware she'd broken through his defences. He had to stay away from her. This time he wasn't going to apply the love 'em and leave 'em rule he'd used to guide him through his youth. It had no bearing on this situation.

He was going to have to keep a distance between Callie Masters and himself, starting right this moment. Even though his brothers would be thrilled, he wanted to be in control of any romance that came his way.

When he married, he wanted to be in his right mind, not confused as hell. He had the distinct feeling that once Callie Masters got into his blood he'd be a slave to her forever.

Rock shifted and tried to move her from his knee, but she turned toward him and wrapped her slender arms around his neck. She cuddled closer, mumbling something sweet in her sleep.

Gently laying her on the couch, he pulled away from her. He rose to his feet with great determination, but a dreamy Callie pulled him down for a kiss that rivaled the best he'd ever tasted. She was warm, enchanting and forbidden, especially when the tip of her tongue probed his lips for entry.

His arms still pinned beneath her back he leaned over, Rock gave in to the invitation and enjoyed the kiss she was awarding him. She was so sweet, sexy and hot, all he could think of was what ecstasy it would be to sink into her warmth.

He was so lost in pleasure that he didn't hear the kitchen door swing open. Nor did he see the light come on.

"Ahem." Roarke cleared his throat. Rock felt Callie stiffen in his arms, then all hell broke loose.

"What in blazes are you doing, Rock?" Roarke demanded.

At about the same moment Callie became aware of what was going on. Suddenly awake and aware that she hadn't been dreaming, she shoved Rock away, but not before her hand caught his cheek with a crack that echoed around the room and momentarily stunned him.

"How dare you?" she yelled, more angry at herself than him.

"He didn't mean it, Callie," Reese soothed as Roarke dragged Rock from the kitchen. "It's just that he's been locked up in the house for too long. Forget it, please."

Callie felt stunned. As reality flowed back, a flush of embarrassment warmed her face. She didn't need to glance at her nightwear to know what Reese and Roarke must have thought. Grabbing the blanket, she averted her face. "I know he didn't mean it. I'm sorry. It was as much my fault as his. He was simply comforting me. I'm sorry, I must have fallen asleep. I thought I was dreaming." She raised her shoulders, then realized with a rush of discomfort what she had just admitted.

"All right. We'll talk about it in the morning. You're tired. Lay down and relax. I don't want you going out to the trailer in this weather." Reese nudged a shoulder toward the storm raging outside.

Callie had forgotten all about the weather.

"Good night," Reese murmured as he left the kitchen. "Go to sleep now."

Callie lay on the sofa and pulled the blanket over her head, wincing as she relived what had happened. Not only had she managed to totally embarrass herself in front of Rock by being a sissy, she'd almost seduced him. Was she so out of touch with her feelings that she could only express them in her sleep?

Even that wasn't as bad as the fact that she had

swung at him because he had responded to her advances. And to top it all off, she had to blurt out to Reese that she'd been dreaming of Rock. Of all the stupid things to say. Why didn't she just admit that she fantasized over his brother so often she didn't know reality from a dream anymore.

Come on, Callie, straighten out. The last thing you need is to fall for some cowboy. But maybe it was too late already. She really wasn't a flirt. She'd always been sensible when it came to men. Peter had changed that.

Now she doubted every move she made concerning men. What if she made another drastic mistake? Why was she reacting to Rock McCall the way she did? Was she subconsciously rebounding into Rock's arms because he'd given her a little attention and kindness? Oh, what a blasted mess!

With a groan of despair, Callie forced her mind to clear. She'd deal with all this in the morning. It was always brighter in the morning, her mother used to claim. But somehow Callie suspected that tomorrow morning would be anything but brighter, and she wasn't thinking about the weather.

THE NEXT MORNING Rock entered the kitchen hesitantly, not knowing what would be waiting to greet him. Surprisingly, there was nothing unusual, just his two brothers and the Sunday newspaper. Obviously one of them had been to town already. "Any damage from the storm last night?" he inquired, reaching for the coffeepot.

"None that wasn't expected," Roarke answered in

a tone that implied he wasn't finished. "What the devil came over you last night, coming down here and attacking that girl? For pity's sake, Rock, I promised her brother that I'd take care of her. She's been through hell lately and she's pretty vulnerable at the moment. Then you walk in and start coming on to her. What the devil is wrong with you?"

Rock slammed his mug on the counter and turned, fire burning in his usually calm eyes. "I did not attack her, I came down to bring her in from that decrepit old trailer. How the hell was I supposed to know she was in here already? Besides which, she's not a *girl* anymore, and she may well have been vulnerable, but no more than I was. She was the one who wrapped her damn arms around me and started that kiss. What the devil was I supposed to do? I was comforting her. She was the one who forced things."

Roarke pounded on the table, and everyone froze. "Bull! She's not that type. Anyone in their right mind can see that she's not like that. She's an innocent."

Rock leaned across the table and spoke in a very menacing tone. "Well, then, my dear brother Roarke, you've been out on your horse and away from the action far too long. She is anything but an innocent. Don't tell me you haven't noticed that bombshell of a body. And she knows how to use it. Not that she'll get another chance with me. I don't want anything to do with the little jinx."

Rock straightened, then glared from one of his brothers to the other. "There is not and never will be anything between me and that vixen the two of you are so eager to protect, so wipe those looks off your faces."

A red-faced, angry Roarke got ready to retaliate when Reese interrupted quietly. "He's right, Roarke. She told me herself that it was partly her fault and that Rock was just trying to comfort her. Let's drop it, all right?"

Rock grabbed his hat and headed out, leaving his breakfast on the table. He stalked across the yard, glancing at the trailer, ignoring the enticing smells of breakfast wafting toward him.

He went into the barn and saddled his gelding, Golden Bear, then gathered a bedroll and a set of saddlebags filled with camping supplies and swung himself into the saddle. He hadn't been on horseback for almost two weeks, and it felt wonderfully relaxing and satisfying.

He headed for the foothills to the north, to a place he knew was quiet and peaceful. It was a place he could clear his mind and extinguish the animosity that was steadily growing within him.

THE SMALL WATER HOLE was the only one of the dozen here cool enough to soak in. The rest of the thermal pools were steaming hot, narrow and deep. This one was just deep enough to cover Rock's aching butt. Sinking down, he sighed.

The sun was falling behind the mountain. His bedroll was spread out near the fire, the rabbit he'd snared was slowly roasting on a makeshift spit, and a pot of coffee bubbled beside it.

He'd ridden all day to get here. Now that he'd arrived the quiet he craved filled him but did not grant him his peace. She was still there in his mind just as she'd been all day long, soft and vulnerable, snuggled into his lap.

What the hell was the matter with him? Why was this one small woman causing such havoc in his life? Why couldn't he get her out of his mind?

Rock thought back to other women he'd come across in his life. He was no stranger to the whims and wiles of women. But this one was different, special in ways he couldn't name. Perhaps if he just had her once, he'd get her out of his system.

On the other hand, he had an overriding fear that if he *did* have her once, he'd never get her out of his mind or heart. She was marriage and kids and... Oh, boy, he didn't even want to think what else. But the word *love* sat pretty heavily on his mind. And love was something he desperately needed to stay away from.

Love weakened a man, and he had no desire to be weakened by a five-foot-tall vixen. Nor did he want to be wrapped around this female's dainty little finger. *No, sirree, this love business is not for me.*

Rock pulled himself out of the water hole and paced to the fire, turning the hand-built spit and letting the fire heat dry him.

He pushed the persistent image of her away. "I will not get involved. I will not want her!" He cursed as he rose to his feet. Throwing back his head, he shouted his anger and frustration into the surrounding black silence. His howl was answered by the mournful mating call of a lone she wolf.

Rock mumbled a few choice curses as he thrust his legs into the waiting sleeping bag. To hell with the female species. All they did was screw up male hormones and, in general, cause agony. But even as he thought it, Callie popped into his mind all pink and smooth and hot and curled into his thoughts for the night.

Right then, he knew that he was a goner. She'd caught him when no other woman had ever come close—and with so little effort. But he vowed he'd fight her right to the end.

4

CALLIE DARED to talk to the big, sweaty cowboy as he came from the barn several days later.

"Listen, I want to apologize for what happened the other night. It wasn't all your doing, and I know that your brothers have been on your back about it."

The men had started to cut and bale hay today—a dusty, dirty job no matter what the weather. For haying it had to be dry, which usually meant it was hot. The work was heavy, constant and tiring. On top of all that, it was a scorcher of a day.

Rock looked exhausted, filthy with dust, chaff and sweat. A strong scent of perspiration and dried hay clung to him. It was a masculine smell that created a tug deep in Callie's belly. No matter how dirty, smelly and tired-looking he was, Rock still had the ability to affect her.

There was something about a man who did hard, physical labor for his daily bread that Callie found terribly humbling and attractive.

Rock ducked his head under the hose and rinsed the dust and chaff from his hair and neck. Damn, but she looked good, even with the sweat stains darkening her T-shirt in the most interesting places. His body tightened at the thought. As much as he was hot and tired, he couldn't help but be affected by her presence. His blood seemed to swell with hormones or something equally potent and uncontrollable.

She drove him crazy! That body of hers had tempted and teased him more times than he wanted to admit. And yet he knew without a doubt that he'd be in big trouble if he let this woman into his life. The best thing to do for himself was to ignore her. She'd be gone at the end of the summer, and he'd be able to get back to normal.

"Well? Aren't you going to say anything?" Callie finally demanded impatiently.

He'd been drinking in the sight of her the entire time he'd been lecturing himself to stay away from her. Rock shook his head to clear the sensual fog that was smothering him. He was going to have to do something about this uncontrollable desire that kept creeping up on him.

Maybe he'd go down to Klancey's tonight and have himself a few beers. If he was lucky he might be able to chase her out of his mind long enough to find himself a willing woman.

One more glance at her affirmed his decision. His body was beginning to feel heavy, and the need that boiled in his veins was enough to overheat even the strongest of men. It was damn near impossible to maintain any sort of disinterest when she was within two feet of him.

He turned away from her and stared into the foothills. "Seems we can't get along in a civil manner. It would be better if we just agreed to stay away from each other. That way I won't insult you and you won't cause me any more damage."

Callie felt her temper begin to simmer. It had taken a lot of nerve for her to come over and talk to him, and he was brushing her off like she was some irritating insect.

Well, to hell with him, then. Callie turned away without another word. She didn't need him. She didn't even like the man. What she really needed was a night out, some music and dancing, maybe some good old-fashioned flirting. After all, she hadn't been out on her own since she arrived.

After Peter, her desire for fun had been dampened. He hadn't approved of bar hopping or dancing. There was no way she was going to let that traitorous stuffed shirt rule her life from now on, though.

She was single and young and could indulge in whatever pleasures she wanted. She could dance all night! And nothing boosted her spirits like a night on the town.

PINETAR WAS a small town that serviced ten or so thousand people who lived in the surrounding area. The town was surprisingly prosperous, given that it was in the middle of nowhere. It was a small, close-knit community regardless of the large area it serviced. People here knew and cared about each other.

Two churches, a post office, a grocery store, drugstore and two restaurants filled the one end of town. At the other end a small plaza had sprung up, which housed a movie theater, two general merchandise stores, a bank and a doughnut shop. Across the street was the seed mill and the only bar in the area, Klancey's.

Klancey was an old cowboy who had an ongoing battle with one of the town's matriarchs, Abby Lancaster. Abby happened to be the McCalls' closest neighbor, which set them in the middle of the feud. They heard both sides of the argument, but that didn't stop them from frequenting the bar.

Klancey's was the same as always, cool, dark and loud. The same old crowd with one or two newcomers sprinkled in. Rock climbed onto the bar stool as Klancey shoved a mug of draft in his direction. He guzzled half of it, then wiped his mouth on the back of his hand. The mirror over the bar reflected the small band that was setting up. In the corner was the gang of cowboys from a neighboring ranch, the Circle W. He knew them, but preferred his own company tonight.

Klancy paused in his bartending duties to chat. "Heard you fellas are building some new homes up there on Blue Sky. Log homes, ain't it?"

Rock nodded. "Yeah, Roarke has it in his mind that me and Reese should find women and settle down. He figures a new house will be a big attraction in catching a wife."

"Hmm. You looking for a wife, too?" Klancey chewed tobacco, then spat into the brass spittoon behind the bar. The plug hit with a familiar ping.

Rock chuckled and pushed his hat off his brow. "I haven't got any use for women except for maybe one thing." A meaningful leer decorated his face. "Women and marriage are the furthest things from my mind. Women are nothing but trouble. And I don't need any trouble."

Klancey grunted and moved away, wiping down the bar. The band started playing, and before long several couples got up to dance.

Rock finished his second beer and turned to watch the dancing couples with his third in hand. That was when he spotted her.

Damn it all to hell, what in heaven's name is she doing in a place like this, dressed like that? Rock almost fell off his bar stool.

Good Lord, he'd always known she was made of temperature-raising stuff, but this was too much. If those blue jeans weren't the closest thing to being painted on, he was a hobbled mule.

Those legs, which had once stood above him all slim and perfect, were the sexiest things this side of the Rocky Mountains. And then there was that blouse, which was almost indecent as far as he was concerned. The fitted waist emphasized her luscious breasts. Women who had breasts like those shouldn't wear fitted shirts, he decided. It only drove men crazy.

Damn her! He noted that the guys from Circle W had their eyes glued to her. And they weren't the only ones.

Rock got to his feet and pulled his hat over his eyes, then strutted over to her, narrowly beating another cowboy. He grasped her arm firmly, making Callie jerk around with her purse swinging. He managed to deflect the missile and pulled her to the bar.

"Rock, what do you think you're doing?" she demanded furiously in a low angry voice, trying to shake him off.

"I'm buying you a drink, that's what." He signaled to Klancey for two and nudged her onto the stool next to his. "What the hell do you think you're doing? Do you have any idea what those guys out there think you are? Coming in here dressed like that." He made the mistake of letting his gaze rove over her. "How the hell did you get into those? I don't think I've ever seen anything so tight in my entire life. You're asking for trouble in a big way, lady."

Outraged, Callie swung a hand to swat him, gasping at his crudeness. He dodged the blow. "I don't have to sit here and listen to this, cowboy. You don't own me."

She began to slide off the stool as Klancey set the two mugs of draft on the bar. "Well, well, who do we have here?" Klancey stared at Callie with eyes the size of saucers.

Rock felt his stomach twist tighter. There was no reason for Klancey or any of the other guys in the bar to look at her like that. "This here's Callie Masters. She's at Blue Sky with us for the summer."

Klancey raised his eyebrows and met Rock's gaze evenly. Silence. A message passed between the two men, and Klancey nodded slowly. "Nice to meet you, Callie. I hope you enjoy the area."

"I'm sure I will, once I get out and see more of the attractions." She grabbed the mug of draft and smoothly slid from the bar stool, away from Rock and the speculative look of the bartender.

Klancey never took his eyes off Callie as she crossed the floor to a small table near the band, and Rock's eyes never lost that hard, possessive look, either. "Oowee! Now there is one choice piece of woman. Is she gonna be a hard one to wrestle down." When Klancey noticed the glare he cleared his throat and muttered something about Rock being the one man who could do the job.

But as the evening went by, Rock had his doubts about that. His gaze barely left her all evening. She was drinking a lot of draft, but some she only half finished so he lost count. She flirted a bit. And she danced with just about every cowboy in the place.

Rock couldn't help but wonder if she was aware of how sexy she was. She didn't seem to realize how many men in the bar were staring at her. Or how the other women in the place were sizing her up. Some tried to imitate her confident, sensuous walk.

There was so much heat in this place tonight that Rock swore the joint would burn down, and it all seemed to be coming from Callie.

Rock was growing impatient with her when she got a little too close to one of the more pushy patrons at the bar. Decidedly she'd done enough damage and that he'd had about taken all a man could be expected to take, he stood, rammed his hat on his head and stomped to the bar. He took her by the upper arm and said, "Come on, sweetheart. It's time to go home."

Callie looked over her shoulder and scowled at him. "Let go of me, Rock McCall. I'm not your sweetheart or anything else. Leave me alone."

"Callie, I'm gettin' mad. Now, come on. It's time to go. You've had your fun but enough is enough."

Callie turned to face him and glanced from the firm hand he'd wrapped around her arm to his face, which was glowing with fire and intent. She clenched her fist and swung at him, hitting him square in the stomach.

Rock hadn't been expecting it, and she packed one hell of a wallop. His first instinct was to double up in pain but the sound of laughter all around him met his ears. Before Callie knew what had happened, Rock had shoved his shoulder into her middle, and she found herself hanging over his shoulder on her way out of the bar. She struggled against his strength, but all it got her was a bump on the head when she twisted and slammed into the door frame.

IT WAS one of the most embarrassing times of Callie's life.

By the time Rock got outside and put her down against his shiny black pickup, she was fighting mad. "You had no right to—" The rest was lost as his mouth came down over hers, effectively silencing her protests until he let up.

"You can't do this. I can do as I—" Again his mouth came down on hers, this time with some pressure behind it. His fingers dug into her shoulders as he pinned against the truck and slowly eased away from the kiss.

"How dare you, you bully—" His mouth came down again, harder and more insistent. His tongue swept across her lips, prodding for entry.

Callie held her lips firmly together even though her head was becoming fuzzy and her heart was pounding to beat the band. Somehow her hands had crept up to his shoulders and her fingers were kneading at the cotton collar of his shirt. Her breasts were swollen, pressed up against his hard chest. She'd known it was going to be like this with him. That kiss they'd shared in the kitchen the night of the storm had been a harbinger of things to come.

The pressure of the kiss lessened, but Rock slowly continued his assault on her senses. At the apex of her thighs she could feel the hardness of his body, and she knew he was as aroused as she was.

She groaned as she felt the long-forgotten spiral of desire spin to life in her body.

Rock must have felt her relax against him because he took one last taste of her, and this time she didn't hesitate to open her mouth. He slipped into her warmth. Callie squirmed, gasping as he explored with his tongue.

He drew away slowly, looking into her eyes for what seemed like an eternity. His erection throbbed against her and he groaned aloud as she flexed her hips and moved closer. Thrusting against her, he let her feel what she was playing with, and she was stunned by her desire. He dipped his head and whispered in her ear.

"You and I need to have a long talk, lady. Right now all I want is you. I want to hold you close, to feel your naked body pressed up against me. I want to bury this part of me in you so deeply that you'll never forget. And then you'll know." He emphasized his promise with another subtle shift of his hips.

She said nothing, not even when he lifted her into the passenger seat and climbed into the cab beside her. He started the truck and drove toward the ranch, one hand on the wheel, one caressing her thigh. Heat poured from the center of her, and she was sure Rock could detect the scent of an aroused woman.

THE FIT OF ROCK'S JEANS got tighter and his anticipation grew tenfold. He was going to have her tonight. He was going to end the agony, and together they'd take a trip of ecstasy.

"Stop—stop the truck." Callie's urgent voice suddenly filled the cab, and Rock pulled to a jerking stop. Callie was out of the truck faster than a jackrabbit being chased by a coyote. Rock was stunned until he heard the distinct sound of her being sick, and all hopes of the hot evening ahead melted away.

He leaned his head on the steering wheel for a minute, cursing himself and his high expectations. He should have known better than to get his hopes up around the jinx.

He climbed from the truck and ventured over to her. As much as he wanted to, he couldn't leave her like this.

Callie was kneeling on the soft shoulder of the road, hanging her head in what looked like shame. Rock approached cautiously. He'd been in this situation before, and that ditch at the side of the road was just as deep and filled with just as many rocks as the gully they'd tumbled into the night he met her.

"You all right?" he asked into the midnight silence.

"Yeah," Callie mumbled. Boy, was she being paid in aces for her cockiness. Talk about being embarrassed. All her bravado of this evening had gone flying into the ditch with her dinner and the half-dozen drinks she'd downed so defiantly.

Of all the stupid things to do, this was the worst. She'd succeeded in making herself an enormous fool. The whole evening had been a bust. She had not only flirted outrageously, tempted Rock and been subdued by him—and now this. Oh, she was great at the art of seduction! This attempt had disintegrated into her greatest foul-up yet. *Yeah! Masters! Way to go! Get the guy real turned on and then cough your cookies!*

"Come on. Let's get you home," Rock said. "You'll feel better in the morning." With strong hands he lifted her onto her feet. The world spun for a minute, then leveled out, but her stomach took a side trip. Callie pushed Rock away and fell to her knees, disgracing herself again.

"Well, I guess that answers one of my questions. I'll have to do with you what my brother does when one of us is too weak to hold his stomach." Rock scooped her up and plopped her onto several tarps stacked in the back of his truck. He tossed a pail at her from the other side then climbed into the cab.

Callie struggled to keep upright amongst the tarps, tools, pieces of machinery and slices of straw. The road was bumpy, and she was being tossed all over the place. Damn him, how could he do this to her? The nausea was bad enough. Did he have to punish her by driving so fast?

The wind tugged at her hair, whipping it around her face. She pulled it away and grimaced at the glare of headlights fast approaching. *Oh, Lord, this is all I*

*need—a giant-size headache and everyone in the area
knowing I came home in the back of Rock's pickup.*

Frantically, she ducked under the top tarp.

Rock watched her in his rearview mirror. He'd
thrown her in the back out of concern for his new
truck, but he really shouldn't have. But damn it, he'd
just about had it up to his ears with her. What with
that little show tonight in the bar and the kissing in
the parking lot, he was close to losing his mind. He'd
been primed for Callie Masters, and she'd disappointed him. He was more disgusted with himself
than with her. How could he have let himself...

How did he think he was going to ignore her if he
kept getting into these situations with her? He didn't
give a darn about his brothers. He had no intention of
getting married. Ever. Let them go ahead and ruin
their lives, but he was never going to step into that
trap.

By the time they arrived at the ranch, Callie was
sleeping, curled into a ball in the back of the truck. He
debated for quite a while what to do about her. As he
saw it, he could carry her into her camper and put her
to bed. Or he could carry her into the house and put
her to bed. Or he could leave her in the truck and not
tempt temptation. That seemed like the safest bet.

He stared at the bright moon and the clear sky. It
wasn't cold and no rain was expected. He glanced at
Callie. She was all soft and feminine in her sleep. His
groin throbbed to life at the thought of lying beside
her. He turned away. He was better off leaving her
here.

He got all the way to the porch before his conscience got the better of him. There was no way he was going to be able to sleep if he left her in the truck. He'd help her into the trailer then leave her.

Easier said than done.

He drew in a deep breath, bracing himself. She was really something, with her dark hair spread out over the golden straw, the moon highlighting the planes of her beautiful face. Rock almost cringed as the memory of her soft lips filled his mind. Quickly, before his body had the chance to catch up with his thoughts, he lifted her into his arms.

Wrong thing to do.

She curled into the heat of his body and moaned ever so softly. He felt that gentle sound right down to his toes.

Rock's eyes widened and he turned quickly, jumping off the truck and almost racing across the yard with her in his arms. The more he jostled her, the more she curled into him. And without a doubt, his body recalled everything about the soft, feminine body cradled in his arms. He groaned as she brushed against his hardness when he lowered her to the ground and opened the door to her trailer.

"Don't let me go," she murmured as Rock nudged her into the trailer. He practically pushed her onto the bed, avoiding her arms as she reached out to him. He wasn't going to get into that situation again.

He drew in a deep breath, and turned away before the temptation grew overwhelming. Callie curled into a small ball and moaned dreamily. Rock raced out of the trailer, escaping just in the nick of time.

ROCK AVOIDED LOOKING in the direction of Callie's trailer the next morning. He strode across the yard to his truck and got in without a glance at where he knew she lay.

He backed the truck out and headed down the lane into town. He was more than glad it was his turn to go into town for doughnuts and the newspaper. He'd barely slept a wink last night and felt angry with himself.

In town, he saw a familiar truck in the lot at the doughnut shop. He parked and jumped from the truck to meet head-on with Buck Wyman.

"Hey, Rock. How's it goin'?" Buck greeted him.

"Good," Rock replied automatically. "When did you get back, Buck?"

"Just now. We're heading to the ranch. Been traveling all night. Brought me a woman back. Gonna get hitched." Buck nodded at the sleeping woman in the truck. "What about you? I heard you had a battle down at the bar last night with some nubile little thing."

Rock glanced at the ground and kicked a few stones. "Oh, that. Just some little lady who wanted more than she could handle." He saw the knowing look come over Buck's face and wanted more than anything to get away from his old friend's questioning eyes. "I hope that you're real happy with your new lady, Buck."

"Yeah, thanks. But what about you? I heard about the houses you're having built on the ranch. Guess you're gonna have to find a significant other to make it into a home now."

Rock shook his head. "No way. It's one thing to enjoy women. It's a whole different game keeping them. I like a little variety in my life, and besides, keeping one woman happy is more trouble than it's worth."

"Well, I used to think the same way until I met Sandy, here. Once you've met the right one, your entire outlook will change. One day you'll see the light, McCall. Well, I'd best be off and get this little lady home to a half-decent bed. See ya at the wedding." Buck chuckled and drove off with a tilt of his hat.

Rock strode into the doughnut shop with purpose in his step. He purchased two dozen doughnuts and a newspaper.

Back in his truck, heading for home, Rock shook his head. Imagine Buck Wyman getting married. Well, for Pete's sake. Buck had been the original bachelor, the loner, the I-don't-want-anything-to-do-with-women guy, and here he was getting married. Damn, it would take a pretty special woman to get Buck to tie the knot and an even stronger one to make him want to stay. Rock smirked. He wasn't ever going to get caught in that trap.

CALLIE WOKE SLOWLY. Every bone in her body ached and throbbed. She moved her head and felt the world tilt. Her eyes sprang open and slammed shut. *Headache. Oh, Lord, a headache.*

She lay perfectly still and tried to keep the blood from echoing through her brain. Was that daylight that she'd glimpsed?

Callie cringed as memories started to flow. Along with them came the shame and humility of the situation. Tears welled in her eyes. She stopped them. There was no sense in making the situation worse than it already was.

Holding her head, she edged to the side of her bed. Across the narrow distance of the camper, she caught a glimpse of herself in the mirror and stopped. She was fully dressed. What in heaven's name had she done last night? The new blouse she'd worn only once was ruined, with a streak of grease or oil running from one shoulder across her breasts to the opposite wrist. God only knew how she'd gotten that stain.

For all intents and purposes she looked as if she'd had a wild night. Not that she could recall much after Rock had tossed her into the back of his truck. Damn the man.

Well, she'd show him. No more sitting around feeling sorry for herself. Callie stripped off her clothes and reached for her terry robe. A shower was the first thing on the agenda, then a good sleep. Then Rock McCall was going to get more than a piece of her mind.

As luck would have it, Rock was crossing the yard to the barn with his brothers when Callie headed to the shower. He smiled broadly. "Good morning, Ms. Masters. Been in any good fights lately?"

Callie glared at him. "Not any fair ones. But I'll even the score sooner or later. Better stay on your toes, McCall."

She slipped into the shed away from the sounds of laughter echoing around in that big empty space that used to hold her brain.

A FEW DAYS LATER, shortly before breakfast, Rock rode into the yard on his big gelding, Golden Bear. Callie was returning from her morning walk and meditation. She had taken to walking to keep her figure trim and her body fit. Meditating was something she had started doing since her arrival at Blue Sky. It proved to be a successful method of calming the chaos Rock caused in her mind and body.

As much as she tried to ignore how big and brawny he was and how he made her feel, she still had to fight with herself constantly so as not to break down and seduce him. She had finally succeeded in smothering that hot, steamy feeling by replacing it with the need for revenge. Smooth, simple revenge.

She'd planned it well and had waited for the perfect opportunity. That moment was now. It was high time that they got everything out into the open, and a little revenge would never go to waste.

Rock purposely ignored Callie as he passed. The other night had convinced him of the need for extra caution around her. She was too tempting. If he didn't watch out, she'd have him caught in her web before he even knew what happened.

In the barn he removed the saddle and began the job of rubbing down his horse. Annoyed that his mind was still outside with the jinx, he pushed himself to work harder. Still, he wondered how the devil she managed to look so pure and innocent first thing in the morning. There should be a law against anyone looking that good at this time of day.

It certainly didn't help that she wore those clinging bike shorts. They made him think of how she'd felt pressed up against him. And then there was the over-size T-shirt she wore over the shorts. Her full, round breasts held the fabric out from her body just enough for a man to slip his hands underneath without any difficulty.

Rock mumbled to himself, hoping to defuse some of the tension that had gathered at his groin. Putting more energy than usual into the horse's rubdown, Rock pulled his thoughts to the job at hand. When he slipped on a soapy spot as he reached for the sponge and caught himself before falling, he figured *she* wasn't around or he'd have ended up on his butt.

Angry at himself and the rest of the world because he couldn't control his thoughts and urges when it came to one black-haired vixen, he cursed. Many more days like he'd had lately, and he was likely to end up with a knife in his back. He was one ornery son of a bitch, and everyone around knew it. And their tolerance of him was growing as thin as his will-power around Callie.

A chuckle greeted him as he rounded the back end of his horse. Stopping dead, Rock surveyed the scene before him with dread. The jinx stood there impishly holding the hose securely in her hot little hand. Rock glanced from her hand to the devilish look in her eyes and prayed that she wouldn't start anything.

"You sound a little hot under the collar, McCall. Perhaps I can cool you off a bit." Callie lifted her arm and took aim. For days, she'd been seething over his treatment of her. The more she thought about it, the angrier she got. It was bad enough the way he'd treated her in the bar and in the parking lot, but after she'd gotten sick... He would have treated a dog better. The memory of him tossing her into the back of the truck irked her more every time she thought about it.

Besides, he'd all but issued a battle call with that stupid comment in the yard the following morning, and if he wanted a battle, he was going to get one. Right now.

Rock slid around his horse but realized almost immediately that he had made a rather large tactical error. He was conveniently cornered. Callie appeared, laying her hand on the gelding's rump to calm him. She smiled wickedly, knowing he'd discovered the error of his ways.

"My, my, what have we here? A trapped McCall?" She shifted to lean against the wall. "Been to any good fights lately, *Mr.* McCall?"

The battle call had just been received. Rock leaned back and measured his opponent. "Naw, not lately. But from the looks of that bruise on your forehead you have...and lost, at that."

Callie felt the first rumbles of her temper getting ready to erupt. The sight of him and the sound of his voice seemed to have that effect on her. "No thanks to you. I believe I'll have to take my retaliation. Chauvinistic acts are punishable nowadays, McCall."

Golden Bear shifted and whinnied his disapproval at the interruption to his bath. Rock patted the gelding's long neck and murmured to him, but never took his eyes off Callie.

"You started that, Callie. You knew damn well how I'd act if you pushed me too far, but you went ahead and pushed anyway. You were this close to being picked up by that gang from Circle W, and if you had been, you'd be sporting a hell of a lot more than a little hangover, some hurt-pride and a bruise on the forehead."

"Are you trying to tell me that you seduced me out in that parking lot to protect me? Come now, Rock, even *I'm* not that gullible. What other way would you like to attempt to get yourself off the hook?"

"Look, lady, I know those guys from Circle W. They have no respect for women. A woman on the prowl is fair game to them. You're damn lucky I laid claim on you when I did."

His comment froze Callie. Damn, she wanted to be mad at him. "Well, thank you then, but darn it all, did you have to throw me in the back of your truck like I was some dog or something? I ought to slug you for that."

"You're too handy with those fists of yours. One of these days..." He drew a calming breath. Maybe she'd forgotten about the hose. "As for the truck, I didn't want you barfing in it. Damn it, it's brand-new. I haven't even had it two months."

"I've had enough of you, macho man. I owe you for quite a few nasty, underhanded things going on behind my back." Callie lifted the hose, fixing her grip more firmly on the handle.

Rock lifted his hands in front of him protectively. "Now, Callie, stop and think about what you're starting here."

Callie ignored his plea and went on. "Everyone says you're like a bear, McCall. And I'm the cause. I resent being blamed for that. You deserve everything you get." She stepped back and pressed the trigger.

A powerful stream of water hit him square on the chest. "I'm fed up with being called a jinx and being blamed for your temper and clumsiness," she stated as Rock fought off the stream of water, sputtering and cursing.

Callie lifted her arm to spray water into his mouth, effectively stopping any comeback. "I'm fed up with your two-way messages—friendly one moment and cold the next. I wanted to be your friend, but I'll be damned if I'm going to beg you."

Callie blasted him again when he dove for the hose. Stepping back, she watched the fury burning in his eyes. Not that it mattered. She was too far into this to stop now. She'd just have to live with the consequences.

"I'm fed up with you watching me. I've seen you doing it. And I'm angry as all hell that you told the ranch men to keep away from me. You had no right to do that. I can make my own decisions on things of that nature. I know how to handle men." She blasted him once more before he'd recovered from the last blast.

Rock had had enough. He dove, charging her for possession of the hose, but she stood firm in her battle, ducking and twisting as he tried to overpower her. She fought dirty, turning the hose on him several times.

He had to give her credit, because when he got his hands on her she was going to pay, and she knew it...yet she stayed and fought.

He was soaked to the skin. As they fought, spurts of water sprayed out, drenching her too. Her T-shirt was wet and clinging to her ripe breasts so that the lacy design of her bra showed through and implanted itself in his mind. Lord, he was going down for the count, drowning in her sensuality again.

After a fierce struggle, he tore the hose from her hands and threw it to the floor, then stomped it with his heavy foot. He grasped her shoulders and backed her against the wall, lowering his head.

She deserved this...and so did he.

5

HARD, PUNISHING LIPS covered hers. The dark roughness of the act was simply too erotic to ignore. He drove his tongue between her shocked lips, plundering and stroking, until she was in a frenzy. His arms, wrapped around her body, held her still. It was as if he had to touch every part of her through this one contact.

Forget about breathing, this was more life-sustaining. Callie knew she really shouldn't be enjoying this so much. Shaking her head slightly in denial, she pushed at his shoulders, but all he did was lean closer, pinning her firmly against the cool stone that formed the base of the barn.

Large, rough hands dropped to her bottom and pulled her into the hard cradle of his hips. He was gloriously full and erect beneath his tight, wet blue jeans. Callie groaned at the thought of merging her softness with his hardness, but at the same time her brain registered the fact that she didn't want him like this. Not when he was angry and intended this only as a punishment.

She twisted her head and pushed him away. Not that it worked. He continued his sweet assault.

Her memory hadn't been wrong, after all. This was

just as good—no, better than anything she recalled or fantasized.

A current sizzled through his quivering body and slipped into hers, jolting her senses. Never in her life had she experienced anything like this, and she wanted more.

Arching her body against his, she twisted her head so he could have better access to her mouth. He obliged by forcing his tongue between her lips to stroke the sensitive roof of her mouth.

She loved the taste of him, wanted all of him. There was familiarity in the feel of him and in the deep sounds that came from his chest. There was passion and fire and something she'd never come across before, something almost overpowering and frightening.

She didn't dare look into her heart, and she didn't want to listen to that little voice that was urging her to stop.

Rock knew he shouldn't be doing this. He had meant to scare her off, not turn her on. He was supposed to be punishing her, teaching her a lesson for blowing his life apart.

He'd thought of putting her over his knee, but that would have been too terribly tempting. Mouthing off at her never got him anywhere—she was too quick on the rebound. Kissing her senseless seemed to work best with her.

He hadn't expected her to taste so good, though, or to feel so right in his arms.

He felt a fine quivering overtake her body like a chill. He pulled her closer, aligning her body with every hard angle of his. Lord, but she was heaven and hell at the same time.

His body was beyond excited. He was so close to exploding right there and then that if he didn't get himself together pretty darned quick he was going to embarrass himself.

He pulled away slowly, not releasing her but looking deep into her half-closed eyes as if the answers to all his questions and doubts could be found there.

He saw heat and passion lurking there, waiting to be freed. But there was something else, too, something that scared the living bejesus out of him.

He stepped away, then lifted the hose and the discarded sponge. She stood shivering, soaked to the skin. The sun that crept into the barn glistened off her long, wet legs. Her chest was heaving beneath her clinging T-shirt. Dark nipples jutting against the dainty lace made him want to take those morsels into his mouth.

He stepped back farther and looked at her face-to-face. "I want you, Callie. All of you." His voice grated like sandpaper. "If you don't want to give it all, get lost, right now."

Rock dropped his gaze to the lightly tanned strip of flesh across her belly where her T-shirt had ridden up. There was just enough room for his hand between her stomach and the waistband of her shorts, if he laid it real flat against her warm skin.

Desire whipped through him until his heart was pounding in the back of his throat. But then he looked in her eyes, and his heart plummeted to his feet and up to his chest, leaving panic in its wake.

There was so much more in her expression than he wanted to take on, ever. He saw more than wanting, more than sex or chemistry. He saw forever. And *that* did an effective job of dousing the fire of his passion.

Callie stared at Rock. He was big, wet and everything she wanted in a man. He was also angry.

What had started as a way to break down the fierce battle of wills between them had developed into a passion Callie had never before experienced.

It was one thing to fantasize over the man, but totally another to follow through with the action, especially when Rock looked as if he didn't know whether to run or stay.

Returning his solemn gaze, she shook her head slowly and whispered in a hoarse voice, "It would be a mistake, something we'd both regret. I think we should be just friends." Callie turned away when he didn't answer her or move, saying, "I didn't think it would get out of hand like this."

She couldn't decide what was more frightening—what was going on inside her or what she saw in his eyes. She needed to get away and examine her feelings, especially the ones that had just blossomed.

Rock stood soaked and stunned, watching her retreat. Sweet Jesus, what was that all about? He knew he deserved her anger. Her complaints were valid. He had overstepped the boundaries with her.

Thank goodness she'd left when she had or there was no telling where things would have gone. He'd *never* craved a woman in such a basic way, never felt the wild animal lust he had just experienced.

If he had made love to her right then he wouldn't

have been gentle, nor would he have given a thought to taking the necessary precautions. That fact alone shocked him. He'd always been conscientious. In fact, he'd never made love without the barrier of a condom. And here he had almost taken this vixen without a second thought.

What was she doing to him? He needed to get control of himself. He needed to get away from the temptation she presented, to examine these new feelings that had come into his life along with her.

ROCK WAS miles away from the ranch, supposedly fixing fences, but he'd drifted off into his fantasies, featuring one dark-haired jinx. It was the cool steady breeze that jarred him back to reality.

He thought he'd learned not to let her free in his mind, not to think about the way her firm body fit perfectly with his.

Now he found himself miles from civilization, horny as hell and a storm was brewing. This was getting to be an impossible situation.

It hadn't helped one bit that he'd gone to town last night and found himself a willing woman. After a few minutes necking with her, the memory of his heated exchange with Callie in the barn had filled his mind and he'd known he had the wrong woman.

He ended up turning down a more than generous offer from the petite blonde he'd been trying to attract all winter long.

He didn't know what was wrong with him. He'd become obsessed with Callie Masters, yet he didn't even like the woman. Maybe it was just that she'd shown up in his dreams to satisfy him so many times he was beginning to confuse reality with fantasy.

Sweet Jesus, what he wouldn't give for just one night in her arms, one night to live out the fantasies, to rid her from his blood so he could get on with his life as it should be. But that was impossible. Anybody looking at her could tell she was the marrying kind. How could a man want a woman who was so totally wrong for him?

As much as he wanted and, indeed, needed a wife, he knew for sure that he didn't want the emotional involvement a woman like Callie would bring.

He shook his head, trying to dispel that L-word. As far as he was convinced there was no such thing. At least there was no such thing as love that went both ways.

Rock collected his tools, glancing now and then at the dark thunderheads rapidly gathering to the west. He was still mulling over the question of love as he climbed into his truck.

When he was just a boy he'd learned that you don't get in over your head when it came to emotions. Loving with all your heart only led to pain. His own parents had died and left him, hadn't they?

Why would anyone take that risk? No, he wasn't going to allow himself to get involved. With her, it was all just hormones, and hormones could be controlled.

He started the truck and followed the fence line toward the ranch. What really scared him about the situation with Callie was what he felt deep inside. Something in him had come to life—a yearning to protect her and make sure nothing and no one ever hurt her. He felt a distinct warming around the region of his heart and a need far stronger than any sexual need he'd ever known.

He thought about the kisses—talk about sweet dreams and fire! What havoc those kisses had created in his body and mind. When he had to swerve to avoid a grassy knoll, he attempted to pull his mind on track.

He focused on the cattle in the distance, grazing contentedly on the dry grass, oblivious to the approaching storm.

He sighed heavily. They'd had a fair amount of rain so far this season, but they still needed more to keep the crops healthy and productive. A bad storm would do more damage than good, though. He prayed a little for rain and Mother Nature's mercy as he drove.

A glance in the rearview mirror told him he'd outdriven the storm. It had veered off to the north, but he knew it would come eventually. He stopped and studied the vast fields around him. He loved this land, despite its faults and fights with man. You could depend on the land. It would always be there. Unlike a woman.

An image of Callie flashed across his mind, and he shook it off. He had to stop thinking about her. He was not going to get involved with her. There was no way he was going to give in to her.

Then he thought about her all the way to the homestead.

CALLIE RODE out to the small crest several miles from the barn, needing the peace and freedom. After sitting at her cramped desk for hours, a ride into the country had seemed like the thing to do. Plus, from here she could see all the buildings on Blue Sky, which would inspire her designs.

For his house, Roarke had chosen a spot at the top of the small hill where the river slowed and widened into a small lake. The land was so beautiful it stirred her soul.

This was going to be a house she would be proud of, with its three screened porches and open concept. The living, dining and family areas would flow into each other, surrounding a massive multifaced fireplace. Roarke had opted for a huge country kitchen, a small office and a sunroom that would hold a hot tub to soothe his hard-working muscles. Upstairs there would be three bedrooms plus a complete master bedroom suite. The woman who married Roarke McCall would indeed have a beautiful home—and a good man.

Why, she asked herself, couldn't she fall for someone like Roarke? He had so many good, solid traits, and she was sure he would treat a woman like gold.

He would never leave her almost at the altar because he'd changed his mind. Nor would he ever blow up at her because of some unfortunate accident. Nor would he ever incite the riot of emotion and desires in her body his younger brother Rock did.

She put a stop to her thoughts at that point, shocked at the direction they were taking. Yes, Rock did do wonderful things to the inside of her, but she was not going to get involved with him. The last thing she needed on this earth was an overconfident, chauvinistic cowboy with an attitude.

Sure, he was handsome. What woman wouldn't enjoy looking at a hunk like him? It wasn't her fault he had deep brown eyes that smoldered all the time. Nor was it her fault he had a hard, broad chest covered in a deep mat of fine dark curls, the mere thought of which made her lose track of all that was going on around her.

Nor was it her fault he wore tight blue jeans that had been washed soft and molded his body perfectly. The sight of his muscular thighs and the intimate cupping of his masculinity threw her off balance every time she watched him strut across that yard toward the barn.

It didn't help one bit that he'd held prime place in her dreams at night, and Lordy, Lordy, the things he did to her in her dreams.

She'd stopped reading all those steamy romance novels before going to bed at night, but it hadn't helped. Somewhere in the deep recesses of her subconscious she'd already installed Rock as her fantasy lover—everything she wanted in a man.

In her dreams he was the perfect husband who brought her gifts of wildflowers and stopped into their home in the middle of the day because he missed her. He would pamper her—rub her feet and back after along hard day, share a bath with her in a huge tub of scented bubbles and carry her to their king-size bed to make slow, exquisite love with her. He would be friend, husband and lover.

And she'd be the biggest fool on this side of the world if she believed that there could ever be a relationship like that. It was just a dream.

Men were all the same, loving and affectionate one moment then disposing of you like trash the next. There was no such thing as true love. There was love for the sake of sex and love for the sake of getting what you wanted. And there was the type of love she'd felt for Peter—the kind of love where you stood behind him and always put him ahead of yourself, a blind, stupid sort of love, all devotion, giving and one-sided sharing. When that kind of love died it left you empty and hurt beyond belief. That kind of love could destroy an able-bodied woman. She would never go there again.

She was free of all that garbage now. It was only recently that she had discovered she was over Peter and had begun to wonder why anyone would want to saddle herself with a man when they could have all this freedom.

Callie settled under a big spreading pine, soaking up the warmth of the sun and revelling.

She laughed at herself, enjoying the life she had now. Who could be more content? It was so beautiful and peaceful and relaxing here. And she didn't need to bother herself with all this baggage. Soon, she drifted into a light slumber and dreams of Rock....

He was beautiful dressed in a tuxedo. Who'd have thought he could look better in formal clothes than in jeans and a cotton shirt? He stood waiting for her, his eyes burning with desire and something she wanted to ignore until later. She knew he would possess her body and soul the first time he took her.

She walked on her father's arm to give herself body and soul to Rock. His gaze was searching, appraising, when she reached him.

He turned to the minister and asked calmly if he might try her out first, then he proceeded to remove her long white wedding gown. He seemed not to notice all the people who calmly looked on, and she found herself standing before the crowd, naked but for her veil and flowers.

"What have you got to give me?" Rock asked as his hands reverently explored her body. She looked into his eyes and whispered, "Only my heart and my love."

Eyebrows raised, he stopped moving his hands and laughed at her. "No, thank you. Don't you have anything else to barter with?" She shook her head.

His laugh echoed through the church, and the crowd jeered as she stood naked and abandoned at the altar. And when she looked at Rock's retreating figure, she realized that Peter was there to greet him at the back of the church. He shook Rock's hand and threw his arm companionably around his shoulders. The two of them left together, laughing.

CALLIE WOKE with a shock as the first drops of rain fell on her and thunder rumbled in the distance. She sat up and dropped her head onto her bent knees. Lord, what a nightmare! What a warning! She rubbed her face, took a few deep, steadying breaths and got to her feet.

If there had ever been a forewarning, that dream was it. There was absolutely no way she was going to allow herself to become involved with Rock McCall, no way.

There was no way she going to give in to his tight jeans and broad chest, she vowed as she mounted her small mare and turned her in the direction of the barn. It was then she saw the rider in the distance. For a moment, she couldn't make out whether he was riding toward or away from her, but he was approaching rapidly, and she sighed with relief. She'd been getting a little nervous about the oncoming storm.

Callie braced herself when she saw who it was. He wore his hat low on his brow, his shirt gaped wide open, flapping in the breeze, as if he'd jumped on the horse without thought. She could see the muscles flexing across his chest, his thighs hugging the golden beast with which he moved as one.

Callie groaned as her body melted like thick honey over a flame. Desire, lust and fire ran through her veins. Doubt battered her thoughts, and she wondered if there was any sense in fighting the part of her that wanted him so badly. Despite everything that had happened between them, she couldn't seem to convince this traitorous body of hers that it wasn't going to get what it wanted.

"What in hell's name do you think you're doing?" Rock shouted as soon as he was close enough to be heard. The rain increased but that wasn't why Callie found herself shivering. It was his raw sensuality and the anger he exuded causing her goose bumps. She didn't answer his demanding question.

He was a stunning figure, one that knocked her off-kilter. Only when he was close enough to hear him mumble some inane comment about dumb city women did she pop from her musing.

"What do you mean? I was out riding when it started to rain. I was on my way back as soon as I—" Before she could finish her sentence, a gust of wind came bellowing down on them. Rock's horse pranced skittishly to the side, but he controlled the great beast with one hand.

Reaching to grab the bridle of Callie's mount, he shouted over the wind. "There's a storm warning out. Couldn't you tell by the sky that we're going to get another doozy?"

Callie glanced around and swallowed hard. As nasty as it had looked when she woke up, the sky now looked twice as bad. Normally she wouldn't have been caught out in something like this.

An ominous rumble of thunder enveloped them. Callie glanced at Rock, knowing her fear was in plain view for him to see. "I...I didn't notice it was this bad."

"Stupid, dumb city woman. Don't you realize you could get killed out in these hills by freak storms? How would your brother like that? Roarke has been out of his mind worrying about you."

Not to say what he'd been through in the past hour since he'd returned to Blue Sky to find her gone.

"Come on. We've got to get a move on before the worst hits. You're already soaked." He shrugged out of his open shirt and wrapped it around her shoulders.

Callie glanced at his naked chest. Dark swirls of chest hair ruffled in the wind. The smooth, hard mus-

cles of his shoulders rippled as he turned his horse toward home.

"Wait. I don't need this. You can't go without your
shirt. You'll catch cold," Callie called over the noise
of the wind.

"Believe me, lady, you need that more than I do. If
I have to look at those nipples of yours much longer,
you're going to be in more danger than this storm
could put you in. Now button that up, and let's go."

"Why, of all the chauvinistic comments and gall!"
Callie sat back stubbornly.

"Don't believe me, huh?" Rock reached over and
grasped the back of her neck. His mouth came down
on hers with a force and hunger that scared her. She
whimpered as he bit into her bottom lip. His tongue
slipped over to soothed the nip.

My Lord, the man is lethal.

Her eyes fluttered shut. Coherent thought deserted
her as she savored the rich, masculine taste of him.
But then the rain began in earnest, pouring down on
them. The horses moved nervously, and Callie whimpered as Rock pulled away.

"It's time...now." Confiscating the reins of her
horse, he led a stunned Callie toward the barn and
her fate. There was no chance of escape, and to be
truthful, she wasn't all that sure she wanted to get
away.

If she hadn't known better, she'd have sworn she'd
been struck by lightning. All her circuits were definitely confused and possibly burned up by the force
of Rock's kiss. He was right. The time had come.

Callie glanced at him through the pelting rain. He

looked wild and sensual on the back of the big horse. Rain slicked his heaving chest.

How could she fight him when he looked like this? He was everything a woman fantasized over. In the eerie light of the storm, he looked like some pagan god astride his mighty steed.

Suddenly, she felt confused. Was this a dream or reality? Once more her gaze roved over his body, then came to rest on his face. No, this was reality. And in that moment, Callie realized the beginning of her downfall. To hell with all the dreams, voices and warnings. She wanted Rock McCall.

The worst that could happen was that he wouldn't measure up to her fantasies. And if he didn't, it would give her more willpower to put him out of her mind. *But what if he does live up to them?* an irritating little voice asked.

GOOD LORD, does she even know how erotic she looks? Rock braced himself and looked straight ahead, knowing that if he allowed his eyes to stray to her he would be drawn in by her hypnotic beauty. And then he looked anyway.

Her dark hair had slipped from the knot at her nape and was blowing around her face and shoulders, caressing her body like a familiar lover. Like he wanted to do. Her lips were swollen from his punishing kiss, and her wide blue eyes were stormy with desire.

She sat perfectly erect, moving naturally with the motion of the horse, proud as a Cherokee maiden.

Sweet fire raced through Rock's veins. His mouth

was drier than he could ever remember it being, and he was hot. Not just warm—hot, as if he was standing in the center of a flame. He wondered if the rain hitting his body was creating steam.

He'd never wanted anyone the way he wanted her right at this moment. He paused to open the gate and turned to her, knowing his eyes betrayed the heat and passion steadily building inside him.

"I want you, Callie Masters, and I'm going to have you. Now." He told her this not knowing whether it was to warn her or what, but he saw what he thought must be fear shiver through her body just before she grabbed her reins from him and cantered across the yard toward the barn.

Thunder exploded, filling the air. Lightning crackled, splitting the low gray sky and electrifying the ground, not once or twice but three times in rapid succession. Rock felt the tension swell in his body, and with a blood-curdling cry he followed Callie at breakneck speed. In his dreams and now, in reality, he intended to have her.

She was in the passageway, slipping the saddle from her horse. His shirt slid from her shoulders to the floor without notice as he confronted her, burning hunger searing him. Grasping her arm, Rock dragged her through the barn, leaving the horses behind. The horses could wait, he couldn't. They were going to investigate this thing that sizzled between them once and for all.

Callie writhed in his grasp as he dragged her toward the stairs. "Just where the devil do you think you're taking me?"

"Up to the hayloft, where we can yell and scream and battle this out and not disturb the rest of the world." He pushed her well-rounded bottom up the steep narrow stairs.

The sweet, rich scent of the dried hay and dust overwhelmed Callie's senses. Long streams of muted light shone through the barn boards with each flash of lightning. Thunder echoed off the foothills to the west, and an eerie silence filled the space between them.

They stared at each other, chests heaving, on the edge, a picture of desire waiting to be liberated.

Callie crossed her arms over her chest and waited. Rock surprised them both by gently covering her mouth with his...so gently. He held her shoulders firmly, but Callie wouldn't, couldn't have walked away from this for anything.

He softly nibbled, enticed and hypnotized, making her want more. More of him, more of the radiating, dizzying warmth of his body.

The air was filled with tension, whether from the electricity of lightning or the storm of desire between them she didn't know.

He drew away, and Callie moaned as he angled his head to better cover her mouth. He tasted her lips thoroughly, teasing, tempting, caressing, coaxing her.

His hand slowly moved under her heavy, tangled hair to stroke the tender skin at her nape.

Callie yielded to the caress, collapsing against him. Sometimes it was better to give in than to fight, especially if you were fighting yourself.

Rock lowered her to the bed of hay on the floor and slipped his hands beneath her T-shirt.

How fantasy paled against reality, she thought. He was bigger, gentler and yet more forceful that she'd imagined. Already his mouth had demanded and given more than she had ever dreamed. Her brain fogged as he pulled the T-shirt over her head. Her breasts strained against the lacy fabric of her peach-colored bra. He bent his head to caress the rounded fullness of her breasts with the tip of his tongue.

Callie gasped and tried to get control of the runaway response overtaking her as he opened the front closure of her bra. Her breasts fell free of their confinement, and Rock caught his breath. His eyes burned.

"Sweet Jesus. You are the most beautiful woman," he muttered in awe.

He caressed each breast, then nipped the tight, hard buds that he had drawn and took them into his mouth. He lavished attention on every inch of her tender, sensitive flesh, mumbling sweet words that neither of them could have repeated later. But the feeling and tenderness raced through Callie's body straight to her heart.

She squirmed, whimpering at the exquisite sensations until she thought she'd go mad. Only then did he take her hand and place it on the long, hard length of his erection that was straining the placket of his jeans.

Her touch was too much. Rock's jeans had become intolerably tight. His breath was harsh and sounded like a freight train struggling uphill. Until she had touched him he had been able to bear the discomfort. But now he was so achingly hard and tight he had no choice but to loosen the pressure.

"Lord almighty, I want you.... You are all I thought you'd be and more. You have burned in my body, and now, at long last..." He pulled his straining zipper down with a loud rasp, releasing the pressure.

Callie gasped at the potency of his desire as it sprang free, protruding far above the low rise of his small black briefs. Her obvious pleasure made him throb even harder, if that was possible.

His bare chest heaved as he stood on one leg and struggled to pull off his boot. Never taking his eyes from Callie, he shifted to the other leg to pull at the other one.

Desperation colored his mood as he hopped around off balance, tugging at the stubborn boot. One more hop to the right and the boot slid from his foot. And Rock disappeared through the floor.

6

CALLIE BLINKED once then twice, not believing what had just happened before her eyes. She sat up.

A loud thump followed by an agonized groan came from below. Pulling on her T-shirt, Callie crawled to the hay-drop hole. Down below, Rock lay on a scant pile of hay. He held his hand over his right eye while one of the horses tugged at the feed he was sprawled upon.

She winced, and a heartfelt oath slipped from her lips.

Rock glared at her.

Callie sat back, rearranged her clothing with shaking fingers, fighting the insane urge to laugh. This could only happen to Rock. She grabbed his boot and tossed it down, and it hit him on the shin. He cursed a blue streak as he lay in the hay trying to do up his pants.

"I had nothing to do with this, Rock McCall!" Callie shouted at him. "And stop your cursing."

"Jinx! That's what you are. A damn jinx. I've been around this barn since I was knee-high to a grasshopper and I've never fallen through one of those damn holes. You're a jinx! Why the hell did I ever think I could straighten out this mess with you? You will always jinx me, lady. Go away and stay away from me!"

Callie bristled. "Fine then!" She would have liked to call him a name, but for the life of her, she couldn't think of one to fit the situation. "Play your juvenile games with someone else. I've had more than enough to do with you, too!" She marched down the stairs and out of the barn, leaving the door wide open.

A gust of cool wet air whipped in across Rock's heated body. He cursed steadily. It seemed he did an awful lot of that lately. He struggled to his feet and wobbled as he attempted to pull on his boot. He looked at the drop he'd just taken. Shaking his head, he muttered in a disgusted voice, "Strike two." Making love to Callie Masters was becoming as difficult a chore as it was to put her out of his head. What a disaster!

THAT EVENING when the earth smelled renewed and the air was heavy but silent, Callie gathered her designs and stepped outside. The sky was overcast, but the breeze was blowing the remnants of the storm away.

She held the finished blueprints of the two houses tightly as she made her way across the slippery lane. She prayed that Rock would not be there this evening, but somehow she knew her prayers would go unanswered.

The back porch light was on, illuminating the path and welcoming her when she felt anything but eager to be sitting down with the McCall brothers.

Reese opened the door as she approached. "Callie!" He ushered her into the dull but cozy kitchen. "I'm glad you didn't get caught in that storm this afternoon. It was quite the downpour."

He glanced out the window toward the hill where he'd chosen to build his house. For a fraction of an instant Callie thought she saw a yearning in him that was almost overpowering.

She wondered if this muscular man who filled the kitchen door was as vulnerable as she was. But that was ridiculous, because nine times out of ten, men were the pain givers, the ones who made women hurt in some way or another. At least, that was how it looked to her.

Roarke entered the kitchen at that moment and went straight to the stove to fill the waiting mugs with coffee. "Have a seat, Callie. Rock will be down in a few minutes. Glad to see you survived the storm. Can't wait until he sees the plans for my house. In the meantime, though, I wanted to talk with you. We're planning on going up to the mountains this weekend. There's some cattle missing and I promised you a trail ride when you first arrived. Would you like to come along with us?"

Callie's eyes lit up. "I'd love to. The weather's supposed to be good over the weekend, and I'd love to see more of Blue Sky. Thanks for asking, Roarke."

"Any time, Callie. It's the least I can do after everything your family has done for me and the fantastic job you're doing on the houses. Have you finished those revisions to the plan we talked about?" he asked eagerly.

"They're done, and if I do say so myself, they are

both going to be fantastic homes. Some lucky women are going to be very happy living in them. Your ideas are great, fair to the woman of the house and considerate to anyone else who may live there or even visit."

Rock strolled in, catching only the tail end of Callie's comment. "Who's coming to visit?" he asked.

He wore his traditional faded blue jeans. These pair was as skintight as all the others he owned. A vivid flash of the moment he'd undone his jeans in the barn and how he'd sprang loose filled her mind. Their eyes met, and Callie blushed, wondering if he was thinking about the same thing.

His shirt was fastened by two buttons, his feet were bare and his forehead sported a nasty purple bruise. But that was minor compared to his eye, which sported a lovely blue-purple shiner. It looked sore and Callie couldn't help but wince.

Rock scowled. Callie looked away, not wanting to feel any sympathy for him. He didn't deserve it.

"No one's coming to visit. Callie was just talking about the houses." Roarke answered Rock's query as he distributed the coffee. He hadn't missed the appraisal on either of their parts. Smiling, Roarke sat between Rock and Callie. His assumption that Callie'd had something to do with Rock's newest injury was right on, and he'd just won an easy twenty bucks courtesy of Reese.

"Okay," Rock said. "Let's see what you've got."

The plans were far better than Rock had expected and like nothing he'd imagined. She was good. As much as he didn't want her to be, he had to admit that. The house suited Roarke. It was big and spacious, and careful consideration had been given to every room and its ultimate use. It was as if she had read his mind, then taken into consideration the place where he was going to build and pulled it all together to make one stunning house.

"This is beautiful. I—I don't know what to say. You did a terrific job here, lady." Rock never tore his gaze from the plans or he would have seen the shocked pleasure on Callie's face turn to a blushing smile. But Roarke and Reese caught her reaction. They glanced at each other and smiled knowingly.

"It's perfect, Callie. Everything I wanted is here. How long will it take?"

"Well," Callie replied in her professional mode, "the ground crew has the base framed, and the cement is scheduled to arrive tomorrow. It will have to set for a week. After that the building crew will arrive and get busy once the materials I ordered have arrived. Hopefully we'll already have the groundwork for Reese's place ready to start by that point. The crew will do indoor and outdoor work at the same time because the weather won't interfere with the work. The men are already putting in longer hours than normal, thanks to the fact that they're staying in the bunkhouse instead of commuting, so you should be living in a new place by summer's end."

"You've got everything well organized, Callie, as expected," Reese stated. "I commend you. It's nice to know that some companies still think ahead for the customer. Now, not to rush or take away from

Roarke's house, let's have a look at what you've come up with for me."

Rock watched every move Callie made for the rest of the evening. Not only was he surprised that she could produce these blueprints, but she spoke in technical terms and sounded as if she knew what she was talking about.

By the time they had gone over the plans and drank two pots of the rich, dark coffee, Rock found himself at awe with her. He was wide awake and eager for more time with her, but she rose to her feet and yawned, daintily of course. She looked tired, and as if all she wanted was to get away from him.

He glanced expectantly at his brothers, wondering which of them was going to stop her from leaving. Neither of them made the slightest move. But he hadn't had nearly enough of her, so he jumped to his feet. "Here, let me walk you across the yard," he volunteered eagerly, too eagerly.

Callie frowned at him. "I'm perfectly capable of crossing the yard myself. You needn't bother."

"Oh, it's no bother. Besides, the ground is uneven and you might turn an ankle or something in the dark." Rock didn't care if he sounded like a beggar, nor did he notice the suppressed laughter and covert glances of his brothers.

Callie pinned him with an impatient stare. "There's nothing wrong with the ground, and I'm perfectly capable of going myself, and anyway, you are the last person I'd want to help me. You're accident-prone." She turned to the other men and bade them a goodnight before stepping into the darkness.

Rock felt like a fool. It didn't help one bit that both his brothers were laughing outright at the rejection she'd thrown in his face.

"Ah, so lover boy has finally found one that isn't so eager to fall at his feet," Reese teased, wiping tears of laughter from his eyes. "Oh, how the mighty fall. If only you could have seen your face when she put you in your place."

"This one will no doubt give you a run for your money, lover boy," Roarke said around a chuckle. "For the first time I believe what you want is not eagerly going to drop into your lap."

Reese went off into another fit of laughter.

Rock stepped onto the back porch. Roarke, who had recognized the determined heat in his younger brother eyes, followed. He spoke in a quiet tone that barely disturbed the peace of the night. "Don't you dare hurt her, Rock. Don't even think about going after her if you haven't any intention of pursuing her to the end. Her brother says she's very vulnerable right now."

Rock swung around and let out a sarcastic laugh. "Vulnerable, my eye. She's the most secure woman I've ever met. You've seen how she treats me. Plus every time she comes near me, I find myself in mortal danger." Absently, he reached up to touch his bruised forehead.

Roarke stared at his younger brother's determined posture. "She *is* vulnerable," he insisted. "She was left standing at the altar seven months ago. She's been thoroughly humiliated. To top it all off, the guy bought the company where Callie worked. Needless to say, he fired her on some trumped-up charge. She's just now starting to come around. So be careful with her. Revenge is all very fine and dandy to heal a sore spot in yourself, but not if it's at the expense of another person's peace of mind. Don't hurt her, Rock. If you really like her, go gently."

ROCK SAT on the porch stairs watching Callie's trailer for a long time that night, thinking about what Roarke had said. It must have been terrible for her to be dumped by the one person in this world she'd trusted enough to commit to in marriage. He felt sick for her and angry at the bastard who had hurt and damaged her. He vowed he wouldn't add to the pain she carried. Probably it would be better just to stay away from her now that he understood her a bit better. So why did he feel even more strongly about wanting her?

CALLIE STOOD in the group of trees that would surround Reese's house at the back, watching the men clean up and leave after the last of the cement foundation was poured. When Rock appeared she realized it was the first time she had seen him in two weeks. Two miserable weeks during which she'd had to live with her guilt over the insult she'd delivered to him. She'd missed him and had been terribly distracted by his disappearance.

Some gentle prodding of his brothers revealed that Rock had been out at the farthest camp in the mountains doing repair work and checking boundary fences. Lord, she'd missed his masculine beauty and his forceful presence. His reappearance caused her heart to leap and her spirits to soar, much to her chagrin.

Was it her imagination or did he seem taller, more masculine, rougher and more exciting? After looking her fill, Callie approached him, stifling her silly reaction to him. "Hi, stranger, nice to see you back," she said.

Rock swung around. He was caught off guard, and his heart fell to his feet then snapped into place with a double whammy. All his resolve to avoid her disappeared. "Hi, there, Jinx, how are you? You look tired." He drank in the sight of her.

"You look tired yourself. Did you get all your work done?" She was praying for peace between them, anything to keep this conversation going.

"Ah, yeah, I did all I had to get done. Ah..." He hesitated as he looked at her. *Oh, Lord I'm down for the count. Those eyes, those lips...* His breath caught as he thought he saw desire flicker in her eyes, but it just as quickly disappeared leaving him to wonder if it was all his imagination. He turned to the foundation. "You've done a lot while I was gone. Obviously everything has gone well?"

"Yes," she replied, feeling disappointed at his reaction and angry at herself for wasting so much time and energy thinking about this man. Would she never learn?

Rock could see the change in her right before his eyes. She'd gone from welcoming to disdainful and he hated it. With a feeling of urgency he tried to prevent her retreat.

"I missed you, Jinx." His hand wrapped around the back of her neck, he kissed her roughly, possessively.

His mouth twisted as his tongue conducted its own sweet type of punishment. He knew as surely as he'd denied it for days, weeks, that he was lost to this woman as he'd never been lost before. Sweeter than sin and oh, so very responsive, she felt like home. She was honey, fresh mountain mornings and...*love?*

He drew back with shock and stared into her heart-shaped face. This was too much, far too much. She was the last woman he'd ever expected to fall in— Lord, he couldn't even *think* the word. It just couldn't be!

Rock was shaking his head and his face was a classic picture of desperate denial.

Callie's heart plummeted. She had warned herself over and over. And once more she silently repeated the litany. *I will not get involved with this man.* She wasn't stupid.

Although she truly didn't understand it, she knew he was about to hurt her. She had seen the dismay on his face just as surely as she had felt his eager arousal when he'd kissed her. She knew the ease with which he could seduce her, and she'd vowed not to give him the opportunity again. As if echoing her thoughts, he took a step backward and muttered a resounding "No."

How dare he! Callie struck out at him, her hand quick to retaliate and bruising in its intent. The sound of the slap to his cheek echoed around the cleared glen, destroying the peace she'd been enjoying.

"What the hell did you do that for?" Rock demanded, rubbing his flaming cheek.

"I only gave what you deserve. Take your 'no' and your shocked expression and stuff it. I'm not one of your many conquests, Rock McCall. I expect to be treated as an equal, not as some floozy you can maul whenever the urge strikes. From now on, keep your hands and your mouth off of me." She turned on her heel and stomped away.

"Well, of all the... You enjoyed that as much as I did, lady! You're just too chicken to admit it," Rock yelled after her. "But you'll have to come crawling back on your hands and knees before I ever do it again!"

He rubbed his cheek, mumbling to himself. "Damn women. They're all the same. Friendly one minute, spitting like a cat the next. She wanted that and she enjoyed it. And if I have any say in the matter she'll enjoy a hell of a lot more than that!" Stopping dead, he threw up his hands. What was he saying?

Turning blindly, he ran smack-dab into a big pine tree. He cursed bloody murder as he turned and tripped over an exposed root at the base, falling flat on his face. He lay there mumbling and cursing. And finally gave in.

Roarke and Reese managed to control themselves long enough to go rescue their love-struck brother from self-destruction. But not before Rock roared his intentions from the ground. "Watch out, lady. Here I come, and when I catch you, you'll be sorry!"

His vow was answered by a wicked laugh from the jinx herself, who was halfway down the lane.

Rock growled something unintelligible when his brothers pulled him to his feet. Embarrassed that they had witnessed his insanity, he shook them off and headed into the bush.

He stumbled to the small meadow beside the swimming hole and collapsed against a tree trunk.

He was in big trouble with the jinx, big trouble. But what the hell could he do about it? When he was around her, he hated her. And when he was away from her, he wanted her. What was a man to do?

ROCK WAS AS HARD as a man could possibly get, and without a hope in hell of doing anything about it. It was all *her* fault. Her and her saucy little bottom straddling that saddle like a glove. Whose idea had it been to bring her along on the overnight camping trip in the first place?

They'd been traveling for about four hours with a short rest period an hour ago at the side of the creek. That was when it had all started. She had gone behind a bush and taken care of nature's call, just as all of them had. Then she'd squatted beside the creek and washed her face and hands. The water had run down her neck and disappeared into her deep cleavage. If that wasn't enough, she'd started bending and stretching her lithe little body, first to one side and then to the other, then forward and back. Her shirt rose temptingly along with her breasts.

It was then Rock began to suspect those breasts were unfettered, and the mere thought had done a job on his libido. Then she'd swung herself onto her horse and nestled her pert little bottom into the saddle with a sassy wiggle of her hips, and his mind hadn't been able to function properly since.

It was getting damn uncomfortable to be this aroused for this long while straddling a horse, and his damn jeans were so tight he was sure Reese had shrunk them a size or two the last time he'd done the wash. Strange, he hadn't noticed their tightness when he was getting dressed this morning.

Luckily the camp was not much farther, and there was a nice icy cold stream that ran close by. He could go drown his physical reactions without anyone knowing just how desperately uncomfortable he'd become.

Callie nudged her horse to the right of the group and came up beside them. They had stopped on the crest of the hill they'd been slowly climbing for the past two hours. Her gasp filled the air as she came abreast of the others who had stopped right at the top of a valley. Down below was a sparkling river and the deepest assortment of greens she'd ever seen. There was nothing but trees, rocks, the river gorge and peace. For a moment she felt like a pioneer looking at the promised land. Excitement welled inside her, and freedom bubbled within her, making her feel as wild and undiscovered as the land itself.

"There are parts of this land where human beings have never walked," Reese said reverently.

"Look up there, Callie. To the right, about a half mile up," Roarke said.

Callie rose in her saddle and craned her neck. "Oh! Oh, Roarke, it's beautiful, magnificent. I'm so glad I came," she said, marvelling over the sparkling waterfall that splashed its way over the steep wall of the gorge.

Rock grunted his opinion, but no one took any notice of him. They all recognized he was in another one of those moods and it was better to ignore him.

WHEN THEY REACHED the camp a little while later, Callie slid from the horse and stood clinging to the saddle horn while she adjusted to the aching tightness of her muscles. She hadn't had a real backache in years, and there was no sense in crying over this one. She'd simply have to deal with it the best way she could—a slow, steady walk and then some cold on the aching muscles. Then she needed to lie flat until the soreness disappeared.

She walked carefully in small circles around her horse, pretending to be inspecting and talking to her. If there was one thing Callie hated more than pain, it was pity.

Soon Callie was able to unsaddle the mare. Smiling, she put the animal into the makeshift corral without anyone the wiser to her predicament.

Reese was tending a campfire, unpacking pots and food, preparing for supper. Roarke was at the edge of camp watching the spectacular sunset. A light evening breeze blew in, cooling the hot and weary travelers. Everyone was relaxed. Peace reigned.

Callie stretched her arms above her head and wriggled, relieved to feel her spine straighten without protest. She sighed feeling contented and at home, though she didn't relish the thought of waking tomorrow morning and admitting to these cowboys that her back was out and she couldn't get to her feet. It wouldn't hurt to soak for a bit in the nearby stream, if there was a convenient, private spot.

She approached Roarke quietly, not wanting to disturb his peace. They silently watched the showy display of the sunset and spoke quietly about the ride out. Roarke told her of a deep spot in the stream not far away and at the same time warned her that Rock had already gone to soak his weary bones.

She decided to wait until later.

Later, it turned out, was after they'd enjoyed a succulent meal of steak, campfire roasted potatoes and home-baked beans. Callie ate just as much as the men, which brought out comments of lumberjack appetites and fresh air.

Apparently, the McCall brothers were so used to women who ate like birds that Callie came as a big shock to them. She shocked them further when she pulled the rich ingredients for s'mores from her knapsack.

As darkness set in, deep and complete, Reese got out his guitar and started to strum. He sang along quietly. It was peaceful and relaxing—the perfect way to end the day.

The coals glowed a dark reddish orange. Occasionally, a bright flickering flame would jump at what was left of the wood. The stars were plentiful and shone brightly, accentuating the vast wilderness. Callie loved the feeling, loved the freedom, the wide-open spaces, the newness of this world.

Out here in the foothills there were no man-made sounds. Smog and congestion were only words. Out here you could let your guard down and enjoy being part of it all without a thought to the past or future.

Reese kept on playing, the music gradually becoming louder as he took requests for old favorites. Callie asked him to sing a love song that had been haunting her. It was about a man who was crazy in love with some woman. Reese sang it so expressively and sadly, it could only have come straight from his heart. This was a man in love if she'd ever seen one.

Callie knew without a doubt that if any man loved her even half as much as Reese loved his missing woman, she would indeed be a very lucky lady. Silence followed the last dying note, surrounding them like a cloak. Callie watched Reese struggle to recover from the pain he'd dug up.

He started playing again in a moment. It was a Gypsy melody that spoke to Callie of her Greek heritage, pulling her to her feet and making her move. She reached out and drew Roarke to his feet to dance with her.

She was living the music. It seemed to be in her soul. She held her arms up high and clicked her fingers in time to the music. Her hips swayed as her feet executed the steps she had learned as a child. She laughed as Roarke turned red with embarrassment, trying to imitate her. Rock was laughing at him, so Callie pulled him up to dance along with his brother.

Reese and Roarke cheered as Rock joined in with stilted movements by the light of the fire.

Rock, on the other hand, was finding the whole episode difficult to handle. Was he the only one aware of the way her body moved to the music? Didn't the others notice the way her entire body was involved? The way she was enticing and tempting him?

His groin throbbed to the beat of the music, and he wanted it to go on for hours. At the same time, he wanted her to stop. He didn't want his brothers watching her. He wanted her alone to himself. She was his.

"If I'd known you guys could dance like that I'd have played that hours ago," Reese said.

"I agree," Roarke panted, out of breath from trying to keep up with Callie. "After that, you probably want that cool wash now," he observed. "Rock will you light the lantern and take Callie to the stream? She wanted to wash earlier, but you were hogging it."

"Sounds like a good idea. I could use another soak myself after that ride. I'll just go in around the corner of the stream." Even as he made the offer, Rock didn't know if he was doing it for the sake of his backside or because he wanted her all to himself for a while.

Callie followed Rock through the bush to the stream. The glow of his lantern created a small ring of light around them. The stream looked cold but refreshing, and Callie relished the thought of sitting in it. Rock hung the lantern on a branch that dipped toward the creek, then he backed away.

"There. That should give you plenty of light. I'll be just around the bend there if you need me."

He looked at her hesitantly, and she realized she was nervously gnawing on her bottom lip.

"I don't know whether I like being left alone out here in the darkness. What if a wild animal comes along?" She looked at him with eyes wide and cautious.

"The lantern will keep any wildlife away. You're safe. Anyway, I'll just be over there. I'll come running if you need me."

CALLIE HAD just finished braiding her hair when she heard Rock whistling.

"Are you decent?" he called before rounding the bend.

"Yes," she replied, and heard the rustle of his body moving through the bushes—then nothing. Turning slowly, she caught him staring. "Is there something wrong?" She glanced at her jogging suit. It didn't have any holes, it was loose fitting, and there was nothing in the world sexy about it.

"No, nothing's wrong," Rock replied. "Except that I want to kiss you. I've wanted to all evening."

Callie said nothing. She didn't move as he came near and lowered his head. His lips brushed hers gently, as if he had never touched her before, not like the other times when he had taken her mouth to punish her for his wanting her. Now, he took her like a lover, coaxing and gentle.

Who would have thought her lips could feel so much and that his could transmit so much feeling? The soft brushing of his lips and the touch of his tongue as it ventured into her mouth to deepen the kiss were things Callie knew she would never forget. She let herself relax into his arms and savor this basic pleasure, feeling the pounding of his heart and the heat of his body. And then she came to her senses. This was the man who had denied her.

Callie stepped back, shaking her head. "No. No more, Rock. We've been through all this before. It won't work. We don't even like each other. Let's stop now before it goes too far."

Rock caressed her neck gently then ran his hand down the thick braid that lay over her shoulder. "You're right, of course. You're always tempting me, lady. And when you tempt me, I forget all the promises I've made to myself and then we get so far.... Then it's like we're jinxed."

"That's just as well," Callie replied. "Even you must see that."

"Oh, yeah...sure I do," Rock answered too quickly.

THE CAMPFIRE was still glowing when they returned. Roarke sat nursing a coffee and glanced at them.

"Where's Reese?" Rock asked.

"Gone out walking." Roarke shrugged. "You know how he gets after an evening of singing."

Rock joined his brother at the edge of the fire and poured the last of the coffee into his mug. Callie prepared her bedroll and spoke quietly. "He's in love."

"Who?" asked Rock and Roarke at the same time.

"Reese, who else? You can hear it in his music and see it in the loneliness that surrounds him. He's definitely hurting. Who was she?"

Rock and Roarke looked at each other, then at Callie. "As far as we know its a neighbor girl, but they don't see much of each other. We just found out about his marriage ourselves. She's gone off to find her way in the world, and he's waiting for her to come back. Reese is different. Sensitive, Mama used to say." Roarke turned to face the fire.

"Remember that last fight at Klancey's?" Rock reminded his brother. "The next morning he said something about a woman being the cause of the fight to begin with. I bet someone said something about Melody."

Roarke nodded. "Yeah, that makes sense. Could be others picked up on what was going on between them even though we didn't."

"Callie's right, he is hurting. Callie?" Rock glanced around for her and found her asleep. He sighed heavily, not taking his eyes from her. She lay on her side facing the fire, looking totally innocent. No one would ever guess that she had wound him up and dropped him again just minutes ago. He drew in a deep breath and rubbed a hand over his face.

Roarke let go a low chuckle. "You're as far gone as Reese. And I know the one who's got you tied up in knots."

"Go to hell, Roarke. You don't know anything!" Rock tossed his coffee into the fire.

Roarke shook his head and laughed. He rose to his feet, slapping Rock on the back. "I guess you'll be the first one to fulfill his end of the deal. Looks like that little Cupid fellow got you but good."

7

MORNING IN THE MOUNTAINS was brisk and damp. Callie woke feeling refreshed even though she'd dreamed all night of Rock. She'd given up fighting the dreams. She drew in a breath of fresh air, reached above her head and stretched. Then froze realizing she was about to pay for yesterday.

She glanced around hesitantly, thankful to discover she was alone. All she needed was for someone—namely Rock—to see her incapacitated. If she could just get to her feet, she knew from experience she could probably walk it off. But first she needed some help to get off the ground. If her luck held she might accomplish all this before Rock returned from wherever he was.

Her luck didn't hold. Just then, Rock strolled into camp, his arms filled with firewood. He cast a glance over to where she lay before dropping the load of branches. "Good morning," he said. "About time you stirred. I was beginning to wonder if that little ride wore you out yesterday." As he spoke, he built up the fire, then settled the coffeepot on the metal grate.

Callie stayed where she was, watching him, trying to decide how to handle the situation. Instinctively she knew it would be next to impossible for her to get out of the sleeping bag and onto her feet gracefully.

"Where are Roarke and Reese?" she ventured.

"They've gone to see if they can find some of those missing cattle. They'll be back in an hour or so for breakfast. Are you going to stay there all day or are you going to get up? Coffee will be ready in a minute."

He turned to face her, and Callie winced. She'd have to confess. There was no way she could wait an hour to answer nature's call. "Uh, I have a problem."

"Yeah, what's that?" Rock still stung a little from her rejection last night and didn't really feel like being generous with her this morning. Watching her sleep for the past hour had only served to waken his hormones, and he was in one of those moods where everyone hated him, including himself.

Callie ignored his tone and continued. "When I was in high school, I went on a trail ride with my class outdoor group. There was a bad storm and the guide couldn't find us a suitable shelter. By the time he did, the horses where skittish. I was the last one to arrive at the shelter, and just as I did, there was a huge blast of thunder and a bright flash of lightning. My horse panicked and threw me off. I broke my back in two places. Sometimes it still acts up. This morning I can't move. At least, I can't get to my feet, and I have to get to my feet in order for it to correct itself." She looked at him, waiting as the solution came to him.

Rock stood there looking at her, his thoughts whirling. That was why she had been so frightened of the storm that night in the kitchen. For a moment fury boiled in him at the stupidity of the guide. Still, he was unsure about the situation. "Is this another of your tricks to get me all worked up and then pour cold water on me?"

Tears welled in Callie's eyes. "I thought we agreed to keep our relationship friendly. I'm sorry your feelings got hurt, but this is no joke. Are you going to help me or do I have to wait until your brothers come back to prove to you that this is no game?" Impatience tinged her voice. Still Rock hesitated.

How the devil was he going to help her without touching her? And how could he touch without wanting?

Weighing the pros and cons, he finally shook his head in exasperation. "All right. What do I have to do? I hope I don't have to touch you."

"Well, of course you're going to have to touch me." Callie's voice registered her exasperation. "You'll have to get me out of this sleeping bag and onto my feet, and you can't do that without touching me."

Rock tapped his foot impatiently as he looked at her. He was going to have to touch her...hold her. Sighing roughly, Rock shook his head, knowing he didn't have much choice.

"I hope you're dressed half decently under there because I don't think I could take it if I had to dress you first."

"I'm dressed," Callie assured him. "Come on. Let's just get this thing undone and get me onto my feet. I have to—" She blushed. Lord, she hated having to be at his mercy. But more, she hated the uncertainty and empathy she read in his eyes.

Rock looked away. Damn, he hated the way she chewed on her lip. It made him want to run his tongue over the bite and soothe the ache. His nostrils flared as he drew a steadying breath into his lungs and unzipped the sleeping bag. Her scent assaulted him as soon as he spread the fabric. His body reacted as he feared it would, with full power, no holds barred. *Damn.*

"Put your hands on my shoulders," he said. "I'm going to grab you under the arms, and at the count of three I'll lift you onto your feet."

"Okay. But just don't let go of me until I say so." Her voice wavered as she grasped his shoulders.

He lifted her with ease. She weighed less than one of the bags of feed he hauled around the barn. It startled him to note that she had gone as pale as a ghost when he lifted her. And she was leaning against him, clinging for dear life.

Rock held tight as she stood there, stiff as a board yet shaking like a leaf. He watched her eyes close against the pain he knew she must be feeling. Gradually he felt the relaxation of her body and the strength returning to her limbs.

Finally she sighed. "You can let go now." Her voice was still a little shaky.

"Are you all right?" He hadn't let go—in fact, he didn't dare let go of her. Feeling like a heel because he'd doubted the seriousness of the situation, he tried to make up by overcompensating.

"I'm fine. It just takes a minute." She smiled a wobbly smile for him. "Thank you. I couldn't have done it myself. I should really get moving or I'll tighten up."

Rock let go of her slowly and stood poised, waiting

for her to collapse. She didn't, although she did sway a bit.

After catching her balance, she smiled warmly at him and moved away. "Nature calls. I'll be back in a minute." She disappeared into the bush.

"Don't go too far! Yell if you need me!" Rock called to her retreating figure. After she'd disappeared into the dense green of the bush, he stood waiting and thinking.

He wondered how in heaven's name she lived like this, never knowing if she was going to be able to get up. All because of some stupid guide who probably wasn't qualified to do what he'd been doing.

He recalled the night she had sobbed during the thunderstorm, and now he understood. Strangely enough, all this newfound knowledge about her only made him want to protect and look out for her. She'd had more than her fair share to deal with. The agony of the accident, all the therapy she'd probably had to go through. And then there was this bit with her broken wedding. He felt bad for her, and a pang of guilt flashed through him.

She was such a babe in the woods, and she needed someone to protect her. Why not him?

Rock paced. He was in trouble. He recognized the feelings that had steadily been creeping up on him since she'd arrived. He'd noticed the anger, of course, the heat and the desire. But he'd ignored the more subtle feelings—protectiveness and a deeper attraction than he'd ever experienced before.

Did these add up to love? Sweet Jesus, this was getting out of hand. He'd have to get away from her now or he was going to find himself hog-tied and branded before he could run.

CALLIE AND ROCK sat next to the fire eating bacon, fried potatoes and eggs. Callie sat crossed-legged on a high, flat rock, her back perfectly straight, her smile easy.

"How long has your back been like this?" Rock asked.

"Since the accident. Twelve years. The surgery did help, but it still flares up once in a while. I sat too long on the horse yesterday. I should have taken more rest periods." Callie shrugged and shoveled another forkful of egg into her mouth. This fresh country air made her ravenous.

"Why did you come along if you knew that you'd suffer for it?" Rock looked up, his fork in midair as he spoke.

"Because I like to ride, and my back hasn't caused me trouble like this in years. I thought maybe I was healed. I should have known better, but I still wouldn't have missed this trip. I love this country and the peace." She glanced around at the mountains. "Anyway, I hate to give in. I like to do what I want to do. I just have to make the best of the hand I've been dealt."

"Crazy woman. You could have injured yourself worse." Rock shook his head and finished his breakfast before he spoke again. "You said you had surgery?"

Callie nodded. "Parts of my vertebrae were damaged. Apparently, after I fell, the horse trampled me, but I was out cold. They did surgery and fused parts of my vertebrae, removed crumbs of bone, then screwed me together with a couple of steel rods. It's the parts that aren't fastened together that cause the problem. But what the hell, I can walk and I can talk. So what if I set off the security checks at the airports and if magnets stick to my back? I'm alive." Callie shrugged, her eyes sparkling with devilment.

Rock looked at her with shadowed eyes, his heart aching for her, even though she was making light of it. He knew that she must have gone through a hell of agony and terror not knowing what would happen. "You're very brave to take it so well."

It was Callie's turn to study him. His comment surprised her. "No, I don't think I'm brave at all. I have no nerve any more, and I'm flighty when it comes to making up my mind. It's not all because of the accident, of course. Life's experiences have made me hesitant about certain things."

"Like making love with me?" he asked after a long silence.

Callie met his gaze calmly. "Yes, like making love with you." She glanced away, not wanting to see the look in his eyes. The last thing that she wanted was his pity, and that was surely what she'd get. She couldn't let him inside.

"Then perhaps I'll have to take the decision out of your hands." His voice was dark and knowing. "I can't accept this friendship bit. The chemistry between us is just too strong."

The sound of the others returning drifted through the air. Callie got to her feet and paced to the edge of their camp. Before they arrived, she spoke quietly, as if she might be overheard. "Maybe that's the only way I'll break away from this prison I've made for myself. Maybe once will be enough to cure both of us."

She turned to greet Reese and Roarke, but Rock sat silently, watching her for a long while, wondering if she really meant what she just said.

CALLIE BEGGED USE of the bathtub for a much-needed soak that evening at the ranch. It was pure luxury, and she wallowed in the scented warmth for far too long.

When she finally stepped out of the bathroom wrapped only in a towel, she was surprised to find Rock leaning against the opposite wall in his classic macho-man pose. "Come in here." He summoned her with a crook of his finger.

Callie hesitated, remembering their conversation about lovemaking from this morning. "No, I don't think I should, Rock."

"I'm not going to try anything. I just thought you could use a good massage, and I'm offering to give you one. Come on, I'm not going to do anything bad."

He was so relaxed and nonchalant that Callie followed him, though still protesting. "But it wouldn't look right. I mean your brothers..."

"My brothers suggested it. Anyway they're outside on the porch. Now come on, Callie. Must everything be a war of wills with you?"

"Oh, all right." She followed him into a large, untidy room with a slanted ceiling. Clothes, books and a variety of leather riding paraphernalia crowded every available surface except the bed. Callie lay face-down on the firm mattress as he instructed. His scent welled around her, leaving little doubt in her mind that this was indeed Rock's bed she was lying on. *Don't think about it*, she warned herself.

How was it that she could want him so much yet fear that very want? She felt the bed move and then Rock was sitting beside her. Her response to his near-ness left Callie doubting her wisdom. How had she allowed herself to be persuaded into this situation?

She fumbled for something to say, anything at all. "Don't be frightened of the scars. They don't hurt."

Rock loosened the towel from her back, sighing with relief to see that she wore panties, at least. But he hesitated when he finally did see the long, thin line from her surgery. There was another scar shaped like a half horseshoe, and he shuddered. He hated the thought of her being hurt so badly. Those concerns overrode the fact that she was lying in his bed almost naked, which normally would have driven him around the bend.

Rock had known it was going to be difficult touch-ing her this way. But he'd had no idea just how diffi-cult until she started to make those tiny groans and noises as he rubbed away the tightness and soothed her aches and pains with his strong talented hands.

Every one of those whimpers and groans added fuel to the fire that had been burning long and hard in him for weeks. And he was sure that if she uttered one more sound he'd explode right there. But there were no more sounds or noises. Rock leaned over and found that she had drifted off to sleep.

The soft warmth of her breath caressed his face. Feelings and thoughts he'd never entertained before warred inside him. She was calm and relaxed in the peaceful beauty of sleep, and he wanted to protect her not only from the world but also from himself.

She had been hurt, and sometimes she barely seemed to be keeping her head above water. Rock knew he should let her go and not pursue her any longer. But he wanted her more than he'd ever wanted a woman.

What was he to do? What was all this tenderness and protectiveness he suddenly felt for her? Was it all part of this thing called love? Was he falling deeper and deeper into a chasm from which he'd never escape? Was it time to give in to the inevitable?

He pulled the covers over her body and wiped the massage oil from his hands. Then, before temptation overcame him, he escaped into the hall and closed the door behind him.

"Is she asleep?" Reese's quiet voice came from the stairs.

"Yeah, she must have been exhausted. It sure didn't take long. I guess I'll let her sleep there. I'll use the couch."

Turning, he faced Reese, who was looking at the closed door. Rock saw the sadness Callie had talked about. She was right. Reese was lonely and hurting.

For a moment, their eyes met in knowing surrender. Reese turned and walked away, his quiet words branding Rock's heart. "Grab on to her and hold tight, before you lose her and a part of your soul."

CALLIE FOUND HER WAY down a hidden pathway to a pond nestled in the bush away from prying eyes later that week. She stripped her jeans and top off to reveal the bathing suit she'd put on at lunchtime. All day long she'd thought about a private dip and cooling off, but the construction crew had worked longer than she expected. Now dusk was beginning to close in, and she wanted that swim more than anything in the world.

Heaven, Callie thought, soaking in the coolness, letting the water relax her. If Rock had been there it would have been perfect.

In the past few days—actually, since that morning she'd woken in his bed—she'd decided that for her own peace of mind she had to give this thing between them a chance or forever regret it. The fire that flared between them was too strong to ignore any longer. If she didn't give in to the electricity that sparked between them, she would always wonder.

No sooner had she made that decision than Rock disappeared into thin air. When she'd inquired about him, she was disappointed to find he'd gone to a cattle auction in Montana.

That little bit of knowledge had upset her more than his disappearance. He hadn't told her or made any comments about going away beforehand. But then, why should he? They were hardly friends, let alone lovers. But Callie had assumed they had settled some of their differences and become closer on the trip.

The man drove her batty. He was always on her mind, and thoughts of him distracted her so often she finally gave in and let them have free rein in her head.

Was this what love was all about? Were these feelings of being incomplete when he wasn't here feelings of love? Were the worrying over his travels and the demented jealousy that he might be with another woman all a part of love? Was this warm feeling around her heart love?

ROCK SIGHED. Lord, he was tired. All that traveling exhausted him, although it had been worth it. He had bought the two bulls they wanted. Then a private trip with one of the American ranchers he knew netted him another bull that was even better than the first two.

He'd had plenty of time to think about Callie and to make some major decisions. He'd had almost too much time to think about her. Too much time to want and miss her. And he'd decided to take his chances, just like everyone in this world.

Right now, all he wanted was to hold her in his arms and have a nice cool swim. He headed to her trailer.

Disappointment flooded through him when he discovered she wasn't there. He headed for the pond anyway with the intention of having a good relaxing swim before searching her out to break the stalemate between them.

CALLIE SAT on the opposite shore and watched as Rock stripped down. There was just enough light filtering through the trees for her to see that he was, indeed, as magnificent a specimen of virility as she'd remembered.

She had been too long without a man in her life, she decided then and there. She wanted Rock McCall. Tonight, she intended to get over her irrational fear of getting hurt again and have this man.

Sitting quietly on the stone, she watched him swim across the pond and back. Eventually, he flipped over to float on his back. He drifted lazily in the shallows, watching the sun set and the darkness gather while Callie collected her courage.

By the time he'd swam his fill and pulled on his jeans, Callie was more than ready to approach him. She chuckled in a deep, satisfied tone, then waited as his shocked eyes searched the shadows and found her.

"Callie? What are you doing down here?" He noticed her wet suit and smiled. "Or maybe I should ask how long have you been down here?"

Callie smiled saucily and shrugged. "Oh, long enough..."

"Did you see everything you wanted to see?" he dared to ask. "Or did you shut your eyes and turn your back like a good little girl?"

Callie shrugged and shook her head. She wasn't going to admit or deny what she had or hadn't seen.

"Perhaps I better show you again. I always say don't purchase what you don't first see." His hands went to his waistband and set to work as he approached her. Callie stood and slipped around the pond to meet him halfway. "I say you need to cool off some more." Raising her hands to his chest, she nudged him into the water. But as she pushed, Rock clamped his hands around her forearms and she followed him into the water.

Callie surfaced and headed for Rock, who avoided her by swimming to the other side of the pond. She disappeared beneath the dark surface. Rock waited in anticipation, searching for bubbles or traces to where she was. She came up right beside him before he had a clue she was anywhere near him.

"Welcome home." She placed her arms around his neck and kissed his lips gently.

Her warm, wet body was pressed against his, and Rock felt the immediate reaction. But before he could wrap his arms around her and hold her, she swam away. He dove after her, grabbing her foot and pulling her to him. "What kind of a welcome-home kiss was that?" he asked as he wrapped his arms around her narrow waist. His lips came down on hers.

Heat rose between them where their bodies met and where he was hard against that very female part of her. Already she could feel her body preparing for him. There was no fear this time. Only the desire and need as his tongue slipped past her lips into her mouth.

Callie moaned and welcomed him. Her tongue twisted around his, and their tastes mixed to become the nectar on which they feasted.

Rock edged her away and allowed her to slip down the hard, wet length of him. This time, he vowed, they would finish what they'd started, but he wanted to give her fair warning and a chance to escape before it was too late.

Callie squirmed closer, nibbling at his neck. Rock groaned as he carried her to the edge of the pond then took her mouth over and over until Callie could do no more than want. Anxious to tell him how she felt, she nudged him away, but he fell backward, disappearing into the dark water. Callie gasped, her mouth dropping open in shock.

Rock sat up in the water, fire burning like coals in his dark eyes. He rose to his feet and murmured in a deep, threatening voice. "Okay, lady. I've just about had it..."

Callie relaxed as she heard the teasing note in his voice. He knew she hadn't meant to push him away. "So what are you going to do about it, cowboy?"

"I'll show you." He walked out of the pond like a huge wet monster and stood on the bank discarding his clothes. When his hand dropped to his waistband, he looked at her. "Gonna run?"

"No, I'm still waiting to see what you're going to do about it." Callie stood her ground, although inside she was so hot she feared she'd melt right there at his feet.

His jeans dropped, and he stood magnificently aroused in the bright moonlight that filtered through the trees, clad in the most ridiculous boxing shorts she'd ever seen.

Callie laughed, howled, in fact.

Rock glared at her, then approached threateningly. "What are you laughing at?" he growled.

"Oh...oh. I'm sorry, it's your boxer shorts. No one wears boxer shorts anymore. And that pattern..." She could barely contain her gasps of hysterical laughter.

"Well, cowboys do. Anyway, it doesn't matter about the covering, it's what's inside that counts." He stood very close, and Callie looked down.

"Well, let's just see about that." She reached down between them and took his hard length into her hand.

Her eyes were large and dark, her hand small and cold. Yet her touch was like fire licking at his soul. He couldn't tear his eyes away from her face, so full of innocence and red-hot desire. He prayed that he hadn't misread the situation. Surely she wouldn't back out this time. After all, she'd started it.

Lord, what a situation to be in. Her hand tightened around his swollen erection and traveled the full length of him, then back again. He groaned, not knowing whether he was closer to heaven or hell at the moment. It was pain and pleasure equally mixed.

She smiled at his response. A sultry whisper reached his ears. "I want you, Rock."

He'd died and gone to heaven as surely as she stood here asking. He nodded, then swallowed the lump in his throat. "I want you, too, sweetheart. I've wanted you since the first time I set eyes on you." His voice was a mere rasp.

She tugged away the barrier of his shorts, and he stood gloriously naked before her. His skin was dark, weathered by the long hours he worked outside, except for the area that started low on his slim hips to mid-thigh. The pale expanse only emphasized the rigid male potency of him.

"You are a beautiful man, Rock," she murmured as her hands crept slowly up his hard chest. Her lips met his gently, a caress tickling his lips. Instinctively he wrapped his arms around her, pulling her close.

He returned her kiss with one as hard as hers had been soft. She didn't disappoint him. They stood, lips pressed together in desperation, twisting tongues probing. Both taking what they needed and giving all they had.

Callie's tiny whimper almost undid him as he lowered her to the ground and rolled on top of her, but she held him off.

He persisted until Callie finally gave in.

His tongue met and mated with hers in a dance far more erotic and primal than anything she'd ever experienced. She squirmed beneath his weight, tiny whimpers encouraging him. Rock continued his caressing and touching.

He rolled them over, never slowing in his sweet mating. Callie knew somewhere in the back of her mind that she was in far deeper than she'd ever thought she could be.

She'd thought she knew what lovemaking was all about, but evidently she hadn't even touched on the real thing before. They had only just begun, and already Rock had shown her things about herself she'd never known. There were secret places in her body that quivered with excitement at the simple touch of his fingers.

She wondered what else he could teach her. If she was this excited now, what was it going to be like ten minutes from now? She paused, shivering, but she didn't move from on top of him.

Rock stroked the feathery tendrils of hair that had escaped. "Did I frighten you?" he asked gently.

Callie looked into his passion-dark eyes and nodded.

"I would never hurt you, Callie." He continued gently stroking her back. "You can tell me to stop any time you want and I will," he said as he ran his hands down her shoulders to cup her breasts. His thumbs raked over her aching, full nipples, and she felt them tighten even more. "Do you want to make love with me, Callie?"

"Yes, yes I do," she whispered.

8

IT WAS STRANGE how the world around them had all but disappeared, how the glen contained only them. Somewhere in the back of Callie's mind she heard the evening birds settling in for the night and the leaves rustling, ushering in the darkness. The pungent smell of crushed grass and pine needles beneath them floated up and teased their senses. Yet she was only aware of the musk of Rock's body and the sweet scent of their mating.

Rock tugged her down to meet his lips and took her far beyond any safe measures of control she'd known before. She was dizzy with the rush of her blood and the hypnotic motion of his kisses.

"Oh, love, what you do to me should be outlawed," Rock murmured while nibbling around her ear, then downward to the tiny snaps that held her swimsuit together in the front.

Callie had no control over her body. She squirmed as a molten heat replaced shivery excitement. He bit into the satin skin at the gentle curve of her neck and shoulder, sending shock waves through her body. Her cry filled the stillness as she arched toward him, seeking escape, begging for more.

She surrendered to his overpowering brand of loving, to the haze, to the ecstasy of it all. The cool air nipped at her steamy flesh. Reality surfaced, teased and slipped away, allowing her to sink into the fantasy.

Rock found his way into her swimsuit and filled his eyes with the beauty before him. He was stunned and ever so glad it was his hands cupping her two perfectly full, ripe breasts with nipples so dark and hard they dared his lips and tongue to feast.

She was sweet as warm honey and, large as her breasts were, they filled his hands graciously. He loved the warmth and the weight of them.

A shiver of desire ripped through Callie. The tremor was so strong he could feel it. She whimpered, small, incoherent sounds that drove him crazy. He bent his head and suckled, glad she let those sounds into the open.

He teased and tempted the dark, throbbing peak and then drew the tight areola and finally as much of the delicious flesh as he could get in his mouth, glorying in her reaction as he urged her closer.

"Lord, you are fabulous, Callie. Come closer, my love," he whispered frantically, pulling her over him so he could devour her.

Callie leaned over him and watched the enjoyment in his face as he took the full weight of her breasts. The pleasure she was experiencing was beyond anything she'd dared dream about. He was creating absolute havoc inside her. She fought to hold back the pressure gathering deep in her womb.

Just when she thought that she was surely going to die of pleasure, Rock moved her away. She lay by his side, disappointed and gasping against his hard chest. Her hips jerked uncontrollably against him as he ran a rough but soothing hand down her heated body.

"Not yet, my love, there is so much more you need to enjoy before that. Calm down a bit," he whispered into her ear, kissing her cheek and lips.

Callie was astounded that he'd known she was so close. She'd never had such an observant or considerate lover.

With Peter, she'd been on her own. Whether she climaxed or not was up to her, not him. But Rock obviously took it to be his sole responsibility.

"Stand up, love. There are too many layers separating us. Let me—" Rock helped her to her feet and reached up to undo the wrap skirt she had fastened over her swimsuit. It fell to the ground, pooling like a silken cloud. Callie felt cool and unprotected, standing there in the darkening dusk with her bathing suit hanging around her waist.

She wrapped her arms around her middle as Rock came to his knees. He shook his head slowly. "No, no, don't hide yourself. You are far too beautiful, far too sexy."

Gently pulling her arms away, he caressed the satin length of her. At her waist, he grasped the bunched-up suit with his large hands, then stopped to press one delicate kiss to her tummy. He lowered the suit, uncovering her inch by breathless inch. He gasped his appreciation when she was as naked as he.

With her ample breasts, gently curved waistline and full, flared hips cradling that black thatch of baby soft curls, she was more beautiful than he'd imagined even in his dreams. He thought he'd died and gone to heaven. He placed one kiss on her tummy just below her belly button and another on that silky soft spot just above the curls.

Callie's knees weakened, but Rock held her firmly, edging her to a small outcropping of rock nearby. "Sit before you fall," he whispered, guiding her to the smooth, warm rock. "Let me fill myself with you."

Callie almost collapsed onto the rock. She was shaking with such intensity that for a minute she thought she'd never be the same.

Rock spread her thighs and reverently knelt between them, then cupped her head in his hands and pulled her mouth to his. He came to her and drank of her as if he was starved for the taste of her. Those same lips followed his hands as they made their way downward, covering every inch of her body. Callie cried out at the pleasure he brought and forgot to be hesitant. She let him take, and enjoyed every blessed moment of it.

Only when she felt the heat of his breath and the sharp nip of his teeth at the tender skin of her inner thigh did she become aware of what he was doing. Before she could stop him, his tongue darted out and scorched the delicate skin of her most sensitive flesh in a kiss so intimate she was sure she'd die. The last coherent thing she remembered was her body tightening.

Overtaken with the most terrifying yet pleasurable explosion of feeling she had ever experienced in her life, Callie soared. The husky cry that was his name flew from her lips as she careened to the heavens.

This was the ecstasy everyone talked of, the ecstasy she finally knew.

Floating into his arms, Callie realized with some shock that she and Rock were lying in the grass. She was pressed against him so closely she could feel every curve and nuance of his body intimately. She struggled to say something, anything, but all that came out was garble.

"That good?" Rock smiled, then kissed her gently, slowly. She soon found herself as hot and anxious as before. Her breathing was fast and erratic.

Rock rolled over her, his big body pressing close. Callie stared into his eyes and trembled. He was so big, and she suddenly felt very small. "Don't hurt me," she whispered, knowing that he wouldn't.

"Never, my love, never." He shifted until he was poised at the entrance to her heated core.

She wanted to tell him he was bigger than any lover she had had, but the words wouldn't come. Not when he was this close. "Love me, Rock. Just like that, love me." And she raised her hips to welcome him.

"This is only the beginning, love," Rock said, his voice low and tempting. "Relax and take all of me." He pressed forward, pushing his way into the tight, molten spot she had readied for him.

He held himself perfectly still while she adjusted to his size, then slowly he began stroking her from the inside out. Callie arched to meet each of his thrusts with one of her own. Her sweet, breathless cries of desire filled his brain until there were no thoughts left in him, and no control. He pounded into her, creating a white-hot friction. Her body stiffened, and her long cry of triumph surrounded him.

He thrust once, then again, and filled her with the very essence of his life. Pain and pleasure warred, then he was lost with her in a place where only lovers go.

Callie opened her eyes, her body still rocking in the aftermath. Rock lay beside her, one arm over his eyes, the other across her as if to prevent her from escaping. Slowly his eyes opened, and he captured her gaze in the fast-falling darkness. "I knew it was going to be explosive, but I had no idea... Are you all right? Did I hurt you?" He rolled to his side and ran his hand over her body.

"I'm fine. In fact I'm more than fine. I'm wonderful! I never knew...."

"You never knew it could be so powerful, did you?" he asked stroking her hair from her face. "Don't be embarrassed. I didn't, either. You're a whole new ball game to me, lady. Excuse the pun."

Callie chuckled deep and low. It went directly to that all-male part of him that should have been exhausted, but obviously wasn't. "Let's get dressed and go find a bed somewhere." He rose to his feet like a graceful god, not bothering to hide the already potent need he felt again. He shrugged as her gaze swept over him and paused at the sight of his erection. "I want you again. What more can I say?"

Callie smiled and climbed to her feet. "We better go to my place. It's closer and more private, and we don't even need to get dressed. Race you!"

Rock looked at the tightening power of his body

and at Callie. "Not on your life, lady. Let's stroll back slowly and neck the whole way."

"Sounding better all the time." She linked her arm in his after scooping up their clothes. They began their walk to her trailer, kissing, touching and laughing at nothing.

"You are one sexy lady, do you know that?" Rock nibbled at her neck and grunted as her elbow came in contact with his ribs. "What in the—"

Callie slapped her hand over his mouth and dragged him behind some bushes. "Someone's coming," she whispered.

They squatted silently behind the sparse covering of bushes and listened as Roarke and Reese came closer, then passed them by. In her panic, Callie got a little silly and began to giggle just as the two of them passed, but Rock managed to keep her quiet by kissing her into submission. Once he'd started again, though, it was hard to stop.

She was everything he'd ever dreamed of in a woman—soft, feminine and sexy. How could he resist? He rolled onto his back and pulled her over him. She was like warm silk spread over him in the dark. Her tongue dueled with his. "Oh, love," he murmured into her ear.

"Let's go to my place, Rock. I think the mosquitoes are out." She slapped at her bottom. "Oh! Ouch! They *are* out, and they like the taste of me."

"So do I," Rock said as he gathered their clothes again. He dragged Callie from the bushes and pulled her toward the trailer.

"I thought you didn't want to hurry." Callie laughed breathlessly.

"That was before I figured out how dangerous it can be romping around in the nude with you, giggle puss. Come on, I want you so bad I itch with it."

THE NIGHT THEY SHARED was full of sweet sighs and fire and hands touching, bodies straining to impart messages that could not be said out loud. It was a night full of kisses that took away all thought. Kisses that told of a feeling far too deep to be acknowledged even now.

Moonlight filled the small room, splashing over the bed and their sleek, naked bodies. "Let's slip into the shower and cool off," Callie suggested lazily after they had loved again.

They walked behind the trailer into the shed. Without the lights, Callie adjusted the water and they both climbed in. Rock held her close, enjoying the feel of her small, full body against his hardness.

"Turn around and I'll wash your back," Callie said and did so—three times, because he kept groaning and asking for more.

"I can't understand why I'm so itchy." He turned and pulled Callie close. "But I do know why I'm so hot." His mouth came down on hers, and their tongues tangled erotically. He reached behind and turned off the taps, not letting go of Callie. "Come on, it's time to get back."

"I like the way your mind works." Callie kissed him deeply as Rock lifted her into his arms and made his way to their own spot of heaven.

IN THE EARLY HOURS of the morning Rock got up and dressed. Callie objected fiercely, but he kissed her forehead and whispered, "I have to go, my sweet. I don't want my brothers to think less of you. Anyway, it might get back to *your* brother. Go back to sleep, little jinx. There will be lots of other times for us." He kissed her forehead and lips very gently, then crept from the trailer to the house carrying his boots.

Callie watched him tiptoe across the yard then flopped onto her bed, which held his scent and that of their lovemaking. She had never been quite as happy as she found herself at that moment.

Her thoughts ran wild as she recalled every nuance of their lovemaking and realized that the fear was gone. Rock would never hurt her the way Peter had. Rock was a kind, gentle man. She felt in her heart that he loved her as much as she did him. Even though he hadn't said the words, she knew by his actions and the way he'd worshiped her.

Callie reveled in the knowledge that she had never known love until now. Things would only get better. They were over the rough spots in their relationship. From here on in, they just had to let nature take her course. No, there was no sense in fighting chemistry and such deep feelings.

She drifted off to sleep to dream of weddings and children running around the yard and Rock by her side, loving her.

ROCK NEVER DID get back to sleep that morning. His mind was spinning with what he'd discovered in Callie's arms. Surely he hadn't found the big L? All he really knew was that he'd never felt as if he'd lost a part of himself to a woman before.

It reminded him of what he'd seen in his father's eyes for his mother. The man had been totally devoted to her. All she'd had to do was smile a certain way and his father would do anything for her. He had been besotted to the highest degree, even to the point of following her into death.

That type of love was frightening and something Rock swore he'd avoid. When he got married he wanted to be able to go do his work every day and not think about the woman he'd left in the house. He wanted someone to warm his bed, bear his children and set up a nice home for him to relax in. And he was not going to get any of that with Callie Masters without paying a dear price for it.

But oh, how she warmed his heart and set fire to his body. Her passionate cries echoed in his head, and his body tightened yet again. He scratched his back to distract himself, then moved lower to scratch the itch that was spreading down his leg.

THERE WAS A black sedan in the lane when Callie ventured out. *The doctor's car?* Well, at least she wasn't responsible for him being here this time.

She marched across the yard with the pan of cinnamon Danish she'd made. Roarke had told her to feel free to use the oven in the house, and she knew this was Rock's favorite treat.

When she stepped inside she found Roarke and Reese laughing so hard that she thought that they might fall off their chairs.

"Good morning, Callie." Reese wiped his eyes and snooped under the tea towel into the pan she was carrying. "Oh, boy, cinnamon Danish. I guess I'd better stay and baby-sit Rock this morning. And I'll watch those for you, too."

"Forget it," she teased. "I'll watch them myself. I'd like a few for myself this time. What's wrong with Rock that he needs baby-sitting?" Callie asked casually, slipping the pan into the oven.

Roarke cleared his throat and spoke in a strained tone. "He got into some poison ivy somehow last night, and he's swollen up pretty bad. The doctor's up there with him now. I don't know how he got it. He said he was down at the pond, but I've never come across any poison ivy down there."

Callie knew exactly where he'd gotten it. In that bush where they'd hidden. That had been her idea. So it was her fault again. Her heart sank.

Reese chuckled, and Roarke was losing the fight to keep a straight face. "How the devil does he get into these situations? I mean, most people get poison ivy on their legs, not their rear ends." They roared with laughter, and Callie winced.

"Well, up until now you've been involved in all Rock's misfortunes, Callie. Have you got poison ivy this morning, too?" Roarke teased.

Callie felt herself flush totally red as burning embarrassment ripped through her. "Ah, no, no poison ivy. I've never had it in my life."

Roarke stopped laughing and crossed the room to place his arm around Callie. "I'm sorry, I don't want you to think we blame his injuries on you. We were just teasing. Now we've upset you."

"No, it's all right. I *have* been present at most of his mishaps. I—" Callie stopped when the doctor came into the kitchen. He looked very serious.

"I'm afraid Rock has more than a dose of poison ivy. Seems he's gotten into some poison oak, and he appears to be a little more sensitive to it than most people. I'm going to have to take him to the hospital for some intravenous treatment. We've got to get the swelling down."

"Can I go up and see him?" Callie asked.

"Well, dear, he's getting some clothes on, and he's as miserable as a she bear with a thorn stuck in her bottom. I wouldn't suggest any of you try to approach him. I'll take him into Lethbridge myself. Give the hospital a call this evening and they'll be able to tell you how he is."

"Are there any other side effects we should be concerned about?" Roarke rose to his feet, his brow creased by concern.

"Some people have breathing problems with an allergic reaction like this. With others it goes the direction of blood poisoning. So far Rock seems to be uncomfortable but stable. The hospital stay will insure that nothing comes up."

"How long do you expect him to have to stay in?"

"Oh, probably two, three days. We'll get the swelling and the itching under control and he'll be home by the first of the week. Ah, here's our boy now."

Rock came into the room moving slowly, walking as if someone had scalded everything below his waist. He avoided all of them as he made his way through the kitchen, down the two steps and into the doctor's car where he collapsed in the back seat.

"Rock? Oh, honey, I'm so sorry. I'll be up to see you this afternoon." Callie leaned in through the open door.

"No! Stay away from me! Wherever you are, there's trouble. Just go away and stay away. Don't ever come near me again." He groaned and gritted his teeth as he moved farther into the car.

Callie backed away. Surely he couldn't have meant what he'd said. It had to be his pain talking, no man could go from being the attentive lover he'd been only short hours ago, to the mean-mouthed ogre he was now. She stepped back when Rock hollered to Roarke to keep Callie the hell away from him. He continued to curse and mutter as he settled into his seat. His face was swollen along with everything else, and Callie wondered how a little poison oak could do so much damage.

It didn't take a lot of brains to see that Rock was extremely uncomfortable. He let out another stream of profanity when Reese rolled down the window and slammed the door shut. His spiel ended with some comment about being jinxed.

Hot, painful tears welled behind her eyes as Callie took yet another step back, bumping into Reese. He caught her in his arms and held her as they watched the doctor get into the car and drive away. But by then, Callie had lost the battle with her tears. She broke away from Reese and ran to her trailer, where she cried out the pain of her betrayal.

She kicked herself over and over for being so stupid and gullible. Twice she had trusted her heart to a man and twice she'd been hurt deeply. Only this time, she knew the pain and mistrust would never stop.

It was a quiet knock on her door an hour later that brought her out of her morose reverie. She blew her nose and answered.

"If you have the coffee, I have Danish straight from the oven."

"Oh, Reese." She sighed and opened the door.

He took in her tearstained face and frowned. "Come on out and we'll talk. I think you need a friend," he said.

She hesitated but gave in. "Okay." After gathering the coffeepot and two mugs, she joined him outside in the screened porch. She busied herself at the table, pouring the coffee and making small talk until Reese stopped her with a firm hand on her wrist. "Want to tell me about it?"

Callie stopped and met his gaze. There was a space of silence and an aching lump ready to explode within her chest. She flopped into a chair beside him. "Yes, I'd like that." She wiped away the tears his loving concern had brought out.

"To start with, you're in love with my brother, the big-mouth." Reese suggested, starting the process.

"Oh, no," Callie denied, shaking her head, then stopped at the subtle questioning rise of Reese's eyebrows. "Okay. Yes. I'm in love with your brother. At least I was. Oh, Lord, why do I get myself into these situations?" She looked away, not wanting him to see her pain.

"He didn't mean what he said. You'll see. When he's feeling better he'll come and beg forgiveness."

"I don't know. He was pretty angry—and vindictive." Callie shook her head as she wrapped her hands around her warm coffee cup. "I thought we were past playing those kinds of games like laying on a guilt trip. I can't get into another relationship where I'm always waiting for the other shoe to drop. Maybe it's better to end it all right now before it gets any more out of hand." Callie looked away. "I can't stand to be hurt again." She wiped the dampness from her eyes.

"That's a question only you can answer. But I must warn you. Think very carefully about what you're going to do. You have to live with that decision for the rest of your life. And if it's the wrong decision... If you truly love him, stick it out, and I can almost guarantee you'll be rewarded. I think he's running a bit scared at the moment. This time apart will do you both good."

"Thanks for your caring and your words of wisdom, Reese." Callie grasped his hand, and Reese bent to kiss her forehead.

"Well, I guess I should be going. I want to go up to the foundation of the house after chores and have a look around," he said, then stopped at the door and turned toward the hill where his house—his sanctuary—was being built. "Not words of wisdom, words of experience." And with that, he was gone.

ROCK LAY TOTALLY STILL. He was alive, which was one thing he had to be thankful for. On the other hand, if this day was going to be anything like yesterday he wasn't so sure he'd be happy to have made it through the night.

Yesterday had to be one of the worst days of his entire life—certainly the most humiliating. He'd been subjected to oatmeal baths and the application of soothing creams by the nurses. Which shouldn't have been that bad, except that none of those nurses were over twenty and they could barely keep straight faces when they applied the cold cream to his most private parts.

The poison had travelled through his system like wildfire. He figured that even though he'd only been touched by the weed on his bottom and back, the squirming in Callie's bed combined with the heat of shower they had shared had spread it all over his body. Then his efficient bloodstream had helped spread it to the rest of his glandular areas. But the worst area was the middle part of him—his manly pride and his butt.

He was swollen, tight and irritable. And as if that wasn't enough, he'd accidentally heard some nurses wondering just how he'd gotten into this mess. He was obviously a great source of humor for everyone, including his brothers. Probably Callie was sitting at home having a good laugh, too.

It figured that the moment he decided to let himself get close to her, the old jinx would get busy and bamboozle him again. He doubted he'd get over this soon.

Last evening, Reese had lit into him for hurting

Callie's feelings. But no one seemed to care what she'd been doing to him. He'd thought for a brief moment, when he was in her arms, maybe all those accidents had been just that—accidents. But now he was more than sure it was her. She was truly a jinx. As he'd said to her before, she ought to wear a warning bell to protect the innocent.

He was going to have to forget her. Regardless of how good she was in bed or how she turned him on like no other woman ever had, he was not going to take any more chances with her.

In the dark corners of his mind, though, he knew it was just a convenient excuse to slip out of a relationship he was sure would overwhelm him.

CALLIE SAT in her bathing suit enjoying the warm afternoon sun while going over the plan of Roarke's house. Tomorrow the first crew would put the roof on, and the second crew would start work on the walls of Reese's house.

The building projects had generated a lot of interest in the area. Just today, several area residents had come by to see what was going on. Roarke and Reese had been more than congenial and had shown them around both houses. Callie had kept a low profile.

They expected Rock to come home tomorrow. He had responded well to treatment and wanted to recover the rest of the way at Blue Sky. She dreaded his arrival knowing that they'd have to have this jinx thing out. She didn't want their relationship to end, nor did she want to keep it alive if it was to be plagued with problems.

Callie still smarted from the sting. She had been a fool to fall for him. After all the warnings she'd given herself she'd fallen for a man who was really no different from Peter. Rock, too, had taken what he wanted and then dropped her flat on her face.

She had to admit that Rock had done it with far more finesse. Chauvinist that he was, he'd led her all the way. Even to bed without a thought to birth control, and that was all she needed after her groundless threat to her family about getting pregnant on her own. She couldn't tell if she was safe or not, since her cycle had been off whack for a while. How typical that the man got off scot-free when the woman was left to worry.

Well, it didn't matter. She would deal with it the way she dealt with everything else nowadays—she'd keep a stiff upper lip and a proud stance. Never let 'em see you sweat, that was her new motto.

She didn't need Rock McCall or any other man. She was better off on her own, and as long as she kept drilling that into her head, she'd be all right. She didn't need Rock McCall. But deep inside she died a little, because she knew that if it wasn't Rock McCall, it would never be any man.

9

CROSSING THE YARD the next day, Callie was in the middle of the lane when Reese drove in with Rock. She hesitated, then continued on her way. Then she stopped and watched a very sore Rock step from the truck. He cast a menacing glance in her direction. Callie's heart dropped, and she knew she was never going to be rid of him. He was too neatly embedded in her heart. They were going to have to have it out once and for all, and now was as good a time as any.

She marched across the lane toward the duo, who were slowly making their way into the house. Reese turned when he heard her behind him and flashed her an encouraging smile. "Hi, Callie. Have you come to see old grumpy here?" he teased obviously trying to defuse the tension in the air.

Callie smiled weakly and cleared her throat. "I've come to talk with Rock. Would you give us some time alone?"

Rock jerked around, scowling. "Forget it. I don't want to be left alone with the jinx. Stay right where you are, Reese."

Reese glanced from Rock to Callie and shrugged. "I really think you two need to talk. I'll be outside. Call me when you're ready to go upstairs."

"I'm ready right now. I'm not talking with her,"

Rock yelled, but his words landed on deaf ears. He stared in disbelief as Reese headed for the door.

Callie took a deep breath before she spoke. "I know that you've had a rough time and you're uncomfortable, but we really need to talk about what's going on. It won't take long. This is not my fault."

"Not your fault? Oh, yes, it is, lady. It was you who dragged me behind those bushes. I should have known better than to let my guard down around you." He was disgusted and tired and wanted her to go away before that little-girl pleading look in her eyes got the better of him. "Why don't you just go home and forget anything ever happened between us? It'll be much safer for both of us."

Rock turned, determined to get away from her before she broke him down emotionally. But he misjudged the small step into the living room and tripped. Seeing what was happening, Callie raced across the room. Rock grabbed the door frame just in the nick of time, but not before Callie barreled into him and sent him sprawling. He crashed with a resounding thud, and Callie landed on top of him.

Déjà vu. Rock growled as he fingered his temple. "Jinx! Go away before you kill me!"

FROM THEN ON, things got worse. Callie avoided Rock as diligently as he did her, and both of them were like ugly bears.

"Do you, or do you not want Callie," Roarke demanded, "to build you a house? Now that my place is done on the outside and Reese's just needs the roof and the finishing touches, I'm sure she'd like to get going on her next project."

Rock grunted and continued eating with his head down.

"It's been weeks since you got out of the hospital. You've had plenty of time to sort things out. Why don't you quit being such a stubborn ass and get on with your life? And do something about clearing things up with Callie. It would make things so much nicer around here."

Roarke continued to eat his breakfast. Rock remained silent. "You know, she's contracted to us for the summer, but if you're not happy with her, then we may as well let her get going at some of the other work she's lined up in the area."

Roarke sat back and watched Rock from beneath a heavy-browed frown.

Rock rose to his feet and poured more coffee, mainly because he didn't want his brothers to see the quiet pain he felt when they talked of Callie leaving. He knew that he couldn't have her, but that didn't stop his need to see her everyday. Not that either of them spoke to each other. In the three weeks since he'd been in the hospital, they had been civil to each other, and that was all.

Rock had been thankful to get out of a relationship he should never have gotten into. And so, apparently, was Callie which was rather like a kick in the pants.

Although he'd never wanted to hurt her, he'd assumed she'd be a little more upset. Was he the only one hurting here? Would the ache ever go away? He wouldn't—no, he couldn't admit that he found each day without her harder to get through than the last.

The way his brothers talked about her ability to design and coordinate the building of these strong and beautiful homes didn't help him any. Everyone who came to see the houses was thrilled with her and sang her praises.

Interested glances came her way from every bachelor cowboy in the area. The red-hot jealousy in his soul grew by leaps and bounds, even outweighing his need to forget her.

And here he was clinging to the kitchen counter, aching for her again.

Reese broke into Rock's thoughts. "So do you want her to build your place?"

"Uh, yeah. I've chosen the plans I want and a spot to build on," Rock finally replied.

"Well, then, talk to her about it." Roarke stood and slid his hat on his head. "I'm going out to the west mountain camp to check how those new bulls are doing. And I want you to settle things with Callie today. Be nice to her, or she may tell you where to get off."

Rock placed his hat on his head, adjusting it low over his eyes. If that was all she told him, he'd be lucky. If there was one thing he could read well, it was an angry woman. If looks could kill, he knew without a doubt, he'd be dead and buried several times over by now.

Well, if he had to do it he may as well get it done right away. He walked down the stairs and to her trailer with long, purposeful, loose-limbed strides that belied the fact that inside he was terrified.

Terrified of five foot three inches of sweet fire!

CALLIE WOKE to the sound of pounding on her door. She'd spent a long night tossing and turning and had only drifted off to sleep at dawn. She raised the curtain and saw the reason for both her lack of sleep and the pounding.

She glanced at the long T-shirt she wore as a nightgown and shrugged, then climbed from her bed and opened the door.

"Hi, did I get you up?" Rock acted casual, although this sleep-soft, fuzzy Callie had almost knocked the wind out of him. He tried desperately to ignore the fact that he wanted nothing more than to pull her into her bed and make love to her until she was cleansed from his system. But something told him she was already in his blood, and besides, she'd never let him into her bed.

Callie left the barrier of the door between them for her own good as well as his. She hadn't missed the look in his eyes. He wasn't as good at hiding his feelings as he liked to think. And then there was the heat that filled her body at the sight of him.

"Yes. I should be getting up anyway. I have a new crew arriving today to start the interior of Roarke's house." She yawned. "Did you want something?"

Did he want something? Was that a leading question? Here she was, fresh from bed, looking all soft, warm and sexy, and she asked if he wanted something. *Yes, I want something, damn it!*

"Yeah, I do. Roarke said I should show you the spot where I want you to build. I decided I'm going to need a house, since I can't very well expect any woman to live in that old wreck that we call home right now. I mean..."

"I know very well what you mean, Rock McCall," she answered icily.

He glanced at her, but she'd hidden behind a mask he'd seen many times before. Usually it meant he was in trouble again. What had he said this time? He frowned and tried to recall exactly what had come out of his mouth, but as usual his brain had gone numb once he was within two feet of her.

"Have you looked at all the plans? Do you have any idea what you would like?" Callie asked blandly, not giving away what was going on in her head. She still had her pride left, and she'd be damned if she'd let him take that from her.

He looked at her. "I've chosen one of the plans in the portfolio. No changes, so it should be pretty straightforward. No strain."

Anything she had to build for him was going to be an emotional strain, but she said, "Fine. I'll take a look at the site you've chosen and then I can tell you if it's appropriate to the design."

Rock automatically became defensive. He had expected her to be nasty and unreasonable, and this was the beginning. "Why wouldn't it be? All we have to do is level and build, right?"

"Not quite. You need to choose an area that is relatively level, that's not a natural drainage spot. It has to be accessible for the machinery. It has to have ground around that we can dig in. You also have to take into consideration the way the ground heaves in certain areas. Then there's the water supply and a septic system to think about.

"If you'll just wait a minute, I'll get dressed and we'll go take a look." She stepped into the trailer and shut the door on Rock before he had an opportunity to respond.

She'd seen that look of determination and anger spreading across his face. It meant only one thing—he wanted to fight. And quite frankly she didn't want to fight with him today. It required too much passion, and she was drained of passion lately.

Dressed in her long navy blue shorts and a deep green T-shirt, she slipped a pair of leather hiking boots over green socks and was ready to go. The image in the mirror caught her eye, and she stopped for a second to study it. She looked good. The few pounds she'd dropped lately made the fit of her shorts looser, and she felt sexy in her new leanness.

She thought seriously about changing, then chastised herself. It would be just too bad if he got worked up over her.

THEY WALKED in silence along the pathway beyond the house. Callie always enjoyed strolling around Blue Sky, but walking beside a broody Rock diminished her pleasure.

"How have you been, Callie?" Rock inquired quietly. He knew how she was. All he had to do was look at her and see the dark circles under her eyes to know she was doing about as good as he was. He also knew her answer would be as bland as his would have been if she'd asked him the same question.

If there was one thing they had in common, it was a huge amount of pride. Neither of them would willingly let the other see them hurting.

"Oh, I'm fine. I love the challenge of having more than one house on the go at a time, especially when they're both my designs." She spoke a little too brightly then went silent again.

The sounds of small animals and birds filled a small portion of the emptiness Callie felt inside. At the same time, she was reminded of the evening they'd made love in the hands of nature, by the pond.

Rock stopped and turned toward her, his dark eyes meeting hers, his fists clenched. "I want to apologize for what I said to you, Callie. I know I hurt you badly, and I didn't mean to do that."

She glanced at him then looked away, shaking her head. The last thing in the world she wanted for him to see were the hot tears that welled in her eyes. "You're right. Your words did hurt me. But I think there was more to it than just your words, Rock. I think that you wanted out of the relationship and took the first opportunity available. That hurt more than anything you said." She turned to face him, watching as a dull flush colored his face. This time he glanced away.

"You know, I wish you had told me to my face. I haven't had all that much experience with men, but I fail to understand why men can't be straightforward and just tell a woman. Why did there have to be an embarrassing scene? You could have just told me in private instead of letting everyone around witness my downfall. But then, maybe men aren't capable of doing delicate things like that face-to-face." Callie lifted her eyes and met his gaze again. She knew without a doubt that her pain was showing as plain as day. Willing herself to display only determination and ice, she said, "It's over now. You don't have to worry. What we had was simply a one-night stand...for both of us. As you said, maybe once was enough. Now let's get on with the business at hand."

Rock shivered at the look on her face and shook his head. He'd known he'd hurt her. Lord, he'd hurt himself for that matter. But he hated to hear her reduce what they had shared to a one-night stand. He hated the cool, strong, unapproachable woman she'd changed into before his eyes.

He swallowed the lump in his throat and started walking again. He'd never been put in his place so cooly. Without a doubt he had destroyed their relationship, but that's what he'd wanted, wasn't it?

He stopped in his tracks and turned to face her. "I can't afford to love you, Callie. Love weakens. I saw it happen to my own parents. I don't want to take the chance. I wanted something simple and uncomplicated. And you aren't."

Callie hesitated. What could she say? He'd said he loved her, but couldn't. Love made him weak, and she was not simple. She cast a confused and angry look at him. "You are one mixed-up guy, Rock. People can't choose what type of love comes to them. Love isn't like that. It doesn't weaken, either, it strengthens. It becomes a part of who you are. There is nothing simple about it. You don't have any choice but to fight it off, which I know you've done your damnedest to do. But you know what, Rock?"

She approached him and poked a finger at his chest. "I won't be around waiting for you. I have better things to do with my life. I have no illusions about love. Yes, I've been stung, but, by God, I'll never be hurt the way I've been hurt by you. You need to grow up and face things like an adult and quit being influenced by your childhood impressions." She turned to go, but Rock stopped her.

"Where are you going?" Now that he was with her and had witnessed the full glory of her anger again, Rock wanted more time. He'd think about what she'd said later. Right now he'd do anything to keep her close by for even a few more agonizing moments.

"I thought we came out here to look at my property. You *are* still going to build my house, aren't you?"

"I've got a job to do and I'll do it," she stated in her best business voice.

Rock sighed and headed down the pathway another twenty feet or so. "Well here it is." He indicated an area set well into the bush and backing onto a natural rock wall. Some way down the hill Callie noted a small creek that seemed to come out of the ground, and she suspected it sprang from somewhere within the wall of rock behind them. Blue Sky was full of small underground streams and springs. The view was wonderful and only partly obstructed by a young grove of pines.

It was one of those spots Mother Nature had created for romantic picnics and rendezvous of a very intimate nature. She tried not to think about the number of women who had been brought here and seduced, but she did anyway, and her face flushed pink with the sheer wantonness of the thoughts. She kept her face turned away from Rock for fear that he would guess where her thoughts had gone.

She didn't know how to deal with her anger, so she took refuge in her work. "I'm afraid this site won't do. As beautiful as it is, there are too many factors working against it. There's no use building a house that is going to stand for a couple of hundred years in a place where it isn't suited." She sounded angry and hated herself for it.

Rock struck his impatient pose, his mouth open and his temper showing. "And what, pray tell, is wrong with this place?" he demanded.

"First of all, that wall of rock is unstable, as most *rock* is." She hesitated until she was sure he caught her double entendre.

"Second, there is an underground creek that comes out about twenty feet below us to the east." She waited until he'd located it before she continued. "That usually means a couple things—that this is a natural drainage area, and that the ground under where we're standing is unstable. This is a relatively young grove. We would have to come in from below and consequently destroy much of that young, sturdy growth. Last, you may have a water supply in that spring down there, but if my guess is right, it's probably solid rock two or three feet under us. That would make it almost impossible to dig either a basement or a septic system. You'll have to find another spot,

Rock. There's no way around it." Callie turned and started to walk along the path.

Rock blustered behind her, his temper at a premium. She had knocked his ego one too many times. "I think you're just making up all this stuff because you don't want to build for me. You're frightened that I'll start something up with you again, and you won't be able to control yourself. You're running scared, Callie." He hated himself for stooping so low to get a reaction out of her.

"No, I'm not running scared, Rock. I'm just being sensible. An architect doesn't care to do a half-correct job. These log homes take a lot of work and extra time to build, but once they're up, they last forever. There is absolutely no way I'm going to build one in an unstable area."

Callie shook her head at his scowl. She'd had enough of the fighting and tension between them.

"I have to get back to the other sites and see how things are going. I believe it's going to rain before noon, and I'd like to make sure Reese's house is covered this morning." She started to walk away, but stopped at Rock's next words.

"Run, then. You don't have to worry about me trying to seduce you. You are the absolute last woman on earth I'd ever bed again. I almost understand why that guy left you at the altar. Who would want to have to deal with your quick tongue, your high-handedness and your knack for creating havoc? I'll have someone else build my house."

Callie stood stock-still, her shoulders stiffening as he spoke. His blows were aimed low and meant to maim. When he stopped, she walked away with what little pride she had left, determined once again never to give any man the power to hurt her like this one had.

Inside her trailer, Callie cried long and hard. She'd thought she was past the point where he could hurt her again, but she wasn't. Maybe she never would be.

Unfortunately, she was still stupidly in love with the man and the dream. No matter how often she had warned herself, she'd still set herself up for the pain he dealt. What he'd just said made it clear in her mind. It was over, but it hurt like hell.

When Callie finally pulled herself together, she went to see how the crews were coming along. Thankfully, her foreman had thought about the approaching storm and had managed to get the roof on Reese's house by using both crews at once. They were just setting down to lunch when Callie joined them.

The men were having a good laugh at the story Roarke McCall had been telling them about the reason they were building the log homes. It wasn't the first time Callie had heard the story, but this time it angered her. Imagine getting married and settling down just to stay out of barroom brawls. Shouldn't mature people be able to do this without resorting to such drastic measures? And to think she'd almost fallen into the middle of Rock's life. Had all the sweet words and the night of passion simply been Rock's attempt to nab a wife and do as his brothers wanted?

Had she been played the fool right to the limit? How many more times would she get herself into these one-sided relationships? Would she ever find a man who would love her for no other reason than love itself? Shaking her head, she wished she could escape from the entire scene, if even for a couple of days. She left the house after a quick check that everything was the way she wanted it.

Rain fell on her head and dampened her clothes as she crossed the yard to the trailer. Her thoughts bounced between loving one minute, hating the next. It was ridiculous but she hated the thought of Rock marrying anyone.

One thing was for certain—*she* would not be marrying Rock McCall, or anyone else for that matter.

Callie flopped on the small couch in her trailer and sighed heavily. The rain drummed hard on the roof and became unbearably loud for a few moments. She was tired. Tired of everything.

Perhaps she needed a holiday somewhere far away and exotic. Her life had been in an upheaval for too long. It was time to stop and figure out a few things or she'd forever go on making stupid mistakes.

ROCK SPENT many an hour berating himself for being so nasty to Callie. He could hardly believe the things that had come from his mouth. Never in his life had he struck out with such vengeance. He had never hurt another human being the way he knew he had hurt Callie.

He was haunted by the sight of her shoulders stiffening and the way she moved away from him. It would have taken a careless, unfeeling monster not to see what he'd done to her. He'd made the worst possible mistake in his life and inflicted some irreparable damage. He felt almost ill about what he'd done.

There was something about Callie that made him crazy, and he always ended up saying things to her that he didn't really mean. Now he was going to have to live with the consequences of his big mouth and the nasties he'd tossed at her.

Sitting in the dark on the porch, he thought about her. That was nothing new—he spent most of his time thinking about her. He had to admit she was a trooper. Regardless of her personal life, she'd continued to do her work and supervise her crews with the same indelible spirit he'd always respected.

He'd expected her to run, but she hadn't, and it was pure hell on him. The sound of her laughter across the yard or the sight of her coming from the shower in the shed or her Gypsy music playing in the late silence of the day was sometimes more than he could bear. He was sorrier than she'd ever know about hurting her, but it was probably just as well. Better to hurt her now than to let it go on and half kill her later. Even if it did leave him feeling dead inside.

CALLIE SANK WEARILY onto the chaise lounge and closed her eyes, listening to yet another summer thunderstorm approaching over the range of mountains to the west. She was used to the storms by now, there had been so many. She no longer feared them as she had when she'd first arrived. That was one thing she had to be proud of, as well as the houses.

She took up the small stack of mail Reese had handed her earlier and shuffled through it. Letters from her father, sister-in-law and Alex. A new brochure from a competitor and the newspaper from home. She read her brother's letter first, knowing it would contain more information and less gossip than the two others.

He was pleased about the houses and the four new contracts she'd negotiated since she'd been here. He suggested that she might want to set up an office in the area if business continued to grow. Callie was definitely against that. Being within a hundred miles of Rock McCall was too close.

Alex included the men's paychecks and her own, with good bonuses for all. Callie tossed hers aside. Money was not one of her big problems. She had a fairly healthy bank account and barely any expenses at the moment.

Alex also reminded her of their cousin Marietta's wedding this coming weekend. A wedding she had not planned on attending, but now thought she might, just to get away from Blue Sky.

She had planned on taking some time off anyway, and a weekend at home sounded pretty good. A weekend of partying, shopping and being with her family might be just what she needed to put things into perspective.

When the rain ended, Callie made her way to Roarke's house. Both crews were working there this afternoon. She passed the paychecks out and told them all to take a four-day weekend. The work had gone faster than she had expected and they were way ahead of schedule. The men would probably enjoy getting out of the bunkhouse and home to their families as much as she would.

Callie found Roarke in his office and informed him of her plans. Before she had time to change her mind, she was packed and on the road home.

THE WEDDING was just as Callie thought it would be—typically formal and family oriented. Just as her own wedding was supposed to have been. The bride wore white, and Callie was willing to bet her bottom dollar Mariette honestly deserved to wear the virginal dress.

Callie hated every blasted minute of it. She hated the way her family looked at her sympathetically. She hated the way her father shed tears and squeezed her hand when the couple were pronounced husband and wife. She hated all the gaiety, the suggestive remarks and the whispered comments that reached her ears even though they weren't meant to.

She hated the way her brothers hovered over her and the way they tried to pair her up with a never-ending procession eligible men attending the wedding.

But most of all, she hated the way that Rock's face was on every one of those men, taunting her all evening long.

She drank too much wine and was carted off home and tucked into bed by her overprotective brothers before she could get into trouble.

Her dreams were full of weddings and relatives. In one dream she found herself fully pregnant and standing in front of the minister in her fashionable maternity wedding gown. Her brothers had hog-tied Rock and were holding a shotgun to his head. Her entire crew was standing behind her, taunting and urging Rock to do the deal. And Rock was laughing and swearing that she was the last woman he'd marry. Finally, her brothers let him go and patted him on the back. They left her there to deal with her father and the angry minister.

Callie woke with a start, her head pounding as hard as her heart. Once again, she swore she would never, absolutely never marry any man, especially not Rock McCall. Not now or ever. And the big ache in her heart widened.

What kind of life would that be? She frowned at her silliness. Her life would be the best she could make it, that's what.

CALLIE SAT on the big cedar deck off the back of her father's house, gently nursing a hangover the size of Texas. Thankfully, the house was empty and quiet for a change. It was usually like Grand Central Station on a Sunday afternoon in the summer as the family came to sun and bathe in her father's pool. Perhaps they'd all had too much partying last night, although that was unlikely.

She lay back after swallowing her third headache pill since she'd pulled herself out of bed that morning. It was not a good day. Between haunting dreams and the newspaper article about Peter's recent wedding to heiress Bonita McGlauglin she was feeling decidedly sorry for herself. But when Alex and his wife,

Claire, came around the side of the house, she had no choice but to pull herself together.

Alex bent and kissed her cheek. "Feeling better this morning? You could have just said you didn't want to be there. I would have brought you home. I know what kind of a strain these family things can be."

Callie just smiled. "I was enjoying myself." She turned to her pregnant sister-in-law. "How are you feeling this morning, Claire?"

Claire smiled warmly and updated her. They hadn't had much of a talk last evening. "What's this I hear about you and some cowboy in the mountains?" She sat back, obviously settling in for a long conversation.

Callie glanced at Alex, who avoided her eyes. "What cowboy, Alex Masters? And who told you what was going on?"

Alex had the good grace to look sheepish. "Oh, I've been talking to Roarke, and he told me all about how you and Rock are having a rough time around each other. I just wondered if there was something else going on."

Callie got to her feet and leaned against the railing to look out over the backyard. "No."

Alex looked worriedly at his sister for a few silent moments then wisely changed the subject. "Claire and I just saw Dad and his...lady friend coming out of the motel on the way over here. I take it he stayed the night with her." He spoke in a tone much like Callie would expect her father to use if he'd caught one of his sons doing the same thing.

Callie turned and smiled. "I guess he's pretty taken

with her. I suppose we'll have a new stepmother soon.''

Alex grunted but didn't offer any comment, which was just as well, since her father and his lady friend came through the house and out onto the deck at that very moment.

ALL IN ALL, it turned out to be a nice day. Their father's lady friend was a nice older woman. She displayed a handsome diamond ring and told them they'd be married in the fall. Callie was the first to welcome her into the family, which gave her some brownie points with her father.

Lying in her bed in the dark later, Callie thought of Rock, as she did every night before she dropped off to sleep. Only lately it had been to curse him, not to think of sweet things. She had deflected all the casual comments about her love life and any inquiries pertaining to the three eligible bachelors she was working for. But now she admitted to herself that she felt lonely for the ranch and the big open spaces. The sounds of cattle and the sweet scent of pine that seemed to be everywhere on Big Sky were achingly missing. She was homesick for the place and had to go back to try to work things through. For better or worse, she needed to try once more to reach Rock.

10

ROCK PACED in his bedroom as he had each night since Callie had left for the city. What he'd discovered about himself since she'd come into his life and blown it apart had eaten at his soul for weeks. It was simple to say he didn't like what he had learned.

He was, for the first time in his life, in love. Although he didn't want a woman in his life, he had one. It was becoming almost impossible to live without her. It ate at his soul like acid and set up a battle between his heart and his conscience that would have brought out the national guard if they had been able to find the source of the upset. He was quietly going insane and he saw no hope of any cure.

There was no way on this earth he could even start thinking of marrying Callie. She'd weaken him faster than anything. He'd turn out like his father, at the mercy of a woman. But at the same time the mere thought of living without her left him feeling dull and hopeless.

And there was still this problem of going out and looking for a wife when he was already in love with Callie. *There, I admitted it*. He slumped onto his bed and stared at the water-stained ceiling. When had this room become so small and lonely...so empty?

If only his brothers weren't adamant about him

getting married. He was caught in a trap of his own making because he'd agreed to the idea, thinking that his brothers would soon forget all about it. He'd made such a fuss about it that he'd pay in a big way if he reneged on the marriage bit. He had no choice, but the last thing he wanted at this point in his life was to get involved with any woman, especially within the bonds of matrimony. This was surely what it meant to be between a rock and a hard place.

It was well past midnight when he finally came to a solution. As weak as it made him seem, he had only one hope. He'd look after it first thing in the morning.

UNFORTUNATELY, it only took Rock a few minutes to discover how unreceptive his brothers could be when they had set their minds to something. If the looks on their faces weren't enough after he had voiced his plan from his long night of thinking, their teasing finished him off. He was struggling with some pretty stiff anger that was all but ready to explode if he didn't get some of this junk off his mind soon.

"Look, you don't understand. I want out of all this. I don't want to ever get married, and I don't think it's a very good idea to fool around with something as serious as this. We were all happy before we set up this deal. Let's just forget it. None of us has even been near a bar since we thought up this piece of insanity," Rock pointed out.

Reese frowned. "We agreed that we'd build these houses and fill them." He knew exactly what was bothering Rock and he wasn't going to give him an inch.

"Well, then, you may as well get started on finding a wife for me, because I'm not going to look. I've had enough. I'm not good with women and I don't need to be married in order to find that out." Rock paced back and forth, turning his hat around and around in his hands.

Silence filled the room as Reese stared at Rock. "Well, I guess if I had to choose your future wife, it would be Callie. A person would have to be blind not to see that something has been going on between you two. What happened?" Roarke said nothing, but watched his brother carefully.

Rock froze. "There is nothing going on between Callie and me. And if you insist on pairing me off with her, I'll have to leave the ranch. There is no way I could marry her."

He stomped out of the kitchen overhearing Reese's parting comment. "He loves her deeply. Just like Pa loved Mom. He's running scared."

That evening Rock visited Klancey's and got himself totally plastered. As drunk as he was, when the fighting started he didn't stand a chance. The bartender called Roarke at one-fifteen and told him he'd better come pick up his brother and pay for the damages.

Roarke was anything but pleased, and a barely conscious Rock heard about it the entire way home. The only thing Rock remembered clearly was the light coming on in Callie's trailer as they arrived at Blue Sky. She was back. Thank God!

He'd made an absolute fool out of himself trying to go to her, right then. Roarke hauled him to the house and sat him down at the table. He placed Rock's swollen hand in a bowl of ice water and proceeded to lecture him while pouring black coffee down his throat.

Rock sat with his eyes glued to Callie's trailer the entire time. Finally just as Roarke was about to give up, Rock blurted out his troubles. "I've ruined it all. I've hurt her more than any one person has the right to. She won't ever forgive me for the things I've said to her. And I can't live without her and I don't want to live with her. What a fool I've been." And he promptly passed out.

CALLIE SUPERVISED the last of the work on Roarke's house that week. The interior was almost completed. The kitchen cabinets, trim and interior doors were being installed today, and Roarke was as excited as a kid at Christmas. He had paid her several visits each day this past week, and she had urged him to call an interior decorator friend of hers.

The house had turned out far better that she'd imagined it would. It was majestic in its position overlooking the valley and the small lake, rising out of the hillside as if it had grown there like the natural bush.

She would be forever proud that she had had a hand in designing and building this place. It was satisfaction at its peak—a job not only done well, but done to perfection.

If nothing else, she had proven herself in this project.

Rock was not experiencing the same thrill over the completion of the first home. He had lost all interest and felt there was no use in him building a place because he was not going to marry. If his brothers resorted to pushing he'd leave the ranch.

He was more unsettled than he'd been since he was a kid. The mere sight of Callie had him tied in knots of guilt and desire. It didn't help that he'd managed to fracture his wrist in the barroom brawl the other night. The thought of being in this stupid cast for the next six weeks made him seethe. As if he wasn't already miserable enough. The only redeeming thing was that they were past rounding up the yearling bulls and heifers for the September sales.

Fall was coming fast. He looked out over the hills where the first colors of autumn were decorating the land. Soon they'd be in the grips of another cold, lonely winter, and possibly Roarke and Reese would have women in their lives, and they'd have their new houses. Roarke had been going out a lot lately, all scrubbed and polished, and Reese, too, had been disappearing.

Would he be the only one living in the old house all winter long?

At that moment he caught sight of Callie coming from the shed. Obviously she'd been taking a shower. Her shiny, wet black hair was flowing down the back of her pastel-colored jogging suit. He could almost smell the sweet scent of flowers that was unique to her. She was walking in that straight-backed way of hers and the memory of that morning at camp when she'd had trouble flowed back to him, along with the feelings of protectiveness, and others more desperate.

This was stupid. She was right there, he wanted her, and she had at one time wanted him, too.

He marched over to her trailer thinking only of holding her in his arms again. Noting the piece of wood that covered what used to be the window in the door, Rock knocked.

The door swung open and the handle hit him straight in the nose. He fell back a couple of steps in shock and landed in the waiting lawn chair behind him. It, too, toppled to the ground.

Callie groaned at the scene before her. It had happened so fast. She'd had no idea that he was standing so close to the door.

Grabbing a towel, she hopped out of the trailer and went to kneel beside him. "Don't you dare blame this on me, Rock McCall. It wasn't me who was standing with my nose so close to the door."

She blotted the blood on his face, then held the towel over his nose while she squeezed his nostrils.

"Oh, sweet Jesus," he moaned and laid back. The fight had gone out of him. What was the use?

Roarke and Reese appeared on horseback from around the side of the barn, and Callie called to them. Seeing Rock on the ground, they dismounted and rushed to his side.

The bleeding had stopped, but his nose was swelling rapidly and turning an awful purple-red color. They hauled him to his feet, thanked Callie for looking after him and carried him toward the house.

But not before Callie heard him say. "She got me again."

THE NEXT EVENING, when Callie was returning some baking pans to the farmhouse, they met up again. Rock's nose was swollen and ugly. Callie turned away, not wanting him to see her hurting for him.

"Uh...would you like to stay and talk for awhile?" Rock asked as he sat at the table.

Callie hesitated. She had promised herself she'd attempt to patch up the mess their relationship had gotten into. She glanced at him and nodded. She couldn't help but notice how his face lit up like a child's on Christmas morning.

"I missed you," Rock stated quietly.

"You did?" Callie swung her gaze to meet his. He nodded, then silence filled the kitchen, making Callie nervous. Rock seemed jumpy, too.

"Would you like to go for a walk?" Rock finally said as he rose to his feet.

Callie sighed in relief, "That would be nice."

They walked down the lane toward the road, the silence of the country twilight surrounding them. Callie wanted to talk to him about everything that had happened between them, but the spontaneity of their relationship was gone, replaced by a terribly inconvenient hesitancy. Still she felt as if she had to give it one more try. "I'm sorry about what happened to your nose yesterday, Rock."

Rock reached up to gingerly touch the swollen bridge of his broken nose. He'd thought a lot about this injury and the others he'd sustained this summer.

He knew it wasn't her fault. But then again, why did these things only happen when she was around?

"It's okay. I'll get over it soon enough."

"You don't really believe I caused it to happen, do you?" Callie placed her hands on her hips, which should have warned him that her temper was building. His hesitancy in answering only fueled her anger.

"Well, I—" He never got any further before Callie blasted him.

Shoving him backward, she let him have a piece of her mind. They backed off the lane and into a shallow ditch. Rock stopped her there as he tried to interject some of his own thoughts, but Callie was too heated to let him get a word in edgewise.

"Stop...Callie, stop. Let me..." Rock said, but she ran on like a train out of control. So he did the only thing he could. He kissed her, a long, passionate, lip-softening, mind-blowing kiss. It silenced the verbal attack as well as the physical attack. But as soon as he withdrew from her honeyed lips, she pushed him again.

Rock was feeling pretty lucky when he caught himself and remained upright as Callie charged to the lane and headed toward home. She was finished trying to get through to him.

Rock sighed in relief, pleased that he hadn't fallen into the ditch. But his luck didn't hold out.

Following Callie, he ran right into a black-and-white striped fellow who didn't take kindly to humans in his territory. Suddenly Rock was coughing and backing away as the pungent odor filled his lungs.

"Oh, Lord! Uh-oh..." He coughed and sputtered as the stench permeated his clothing. Every breath he drew in stuck in his chest as he ripped off his shirt and tossed it in the direction of the skunk.

"Damn it, double damn. She's done it again!" Rock climbed from the ditch. "Well, I've had it. I'm through with her. I'm through with all females." He got no farther than a couple of feet when from the ditch climbed mama skunk and her four little ones. They chittered at him with a high-pitched screamy sound. Rock sat where he was and waited. The last thing he needed was a run-in with her, too. And how did he know they weren't all female?

Rock tried just about everything to get rid of the skunk smell before he went to his brothers for help. By this time he was practically sick to his stomach with the odor. But instead of sympathy, he got teasing and laughter. They howled even more when they found out that Callie had been with him. Finally they made up a brew of tomato juice, tomato sauce and catsup for him. Rock sat in the soupy mess and cursed the jinx.

IT WAS TWO DAYS before the smell went away. Roarke and Reese told Callie what had happened, and they shared a good laugh, even though Callie felt bad. Rock McCall was by far the clumsiest man she knew. Just the same, she knew it would be better to stay out of his way for a while.

He surprised her one evening when she wandered

into the barn to feed her favorite mare a carrot. Just inside the door Rock sat soaping his saddle. Callie had no choice but to stop when he talked to her. "Hello, Jinx," he said amicably. "Wanna talk for a bit?"

"No, thanks." She hesitated. "I'm tired from all the packing and trying to get the last of the work on Reese's house done. I'm going to bed."

"Wait! Are you leaving Blue Sky?" he blurted, holding the door open.

She looked straight at him and raised her eyebrows. "Yes. There isn't much reason for me to stay around. The houses are all done except a few interior things at Reese's place. Fall is coming, so there isn't much use in me hanging around. I have some other places to start and I'd like to take a holiday first."

"But what about my—I thought you were going to do my place."

"You decided against that, remember?"

Rock looked at her solemnly, his eyes begging her. "Sometimes you can't have what you want. Sometimes it all gets to be too much to bear and it's no longer worth the strain, is it?"

Callie fought the hot burn of tears and closed her eyes on the anguish she saw in his. "Some lessons you learn and never forget. Sometimes things are prevented from happening for a reason. It's better to say goodbye."

She moved toward the door and walked away from Rock and everything he'd ever meant to her. Sometimes saying goodbye was the only way to peace of mind.

THE SUN WAS WARM, and the sounds of the ocean soothed Callie's nerves. She deserved this holiday and didn't regret spending the money on first-class everything. She was staying at the best hotel on the island of Molokai, sparing nothing to have one blessed week of luxury. She had walked the miles of golden beaches the day she arrived and done little else since except sleep, eat and rest in the sun.

As much as she was determined to forget Rock McCall, his memory had followed her here. There was no escaping him, no matter where she ran.

So this was love. Callie sighed as she sat and watched the sun begin its descent in the western sky. How did a person get over something like this?

Knowing that he was there at Blue Sky, and that she still wanted him, hurt. Why he'd said the things he did and pushed her away she'd never know. She did know that at one time he'd loved her, or at least she thought he had. Maybe she'd been wrong.

He had pushed her away and she had gone, but her heart remained with him. And deep inside he would always be with her. What in heaven's name was going to happen? She was in love with a man who didn't want her. It was time to forget him and stop hoping. But would she ever stop wanting?

Callie hated the unsure wimp she'd become. She wanted to live and be alive again, and to do that she was going to have to put Rock out of her mind.

"Hello. I noticed you sitting out here all alone and decided to come join you. Do you mind?" asked a cultured British voice.

Callie looked up to see a tall gentleman and smiled.

"Go ahead." He was a good-looking man with sandy brown, well-styled hair and a strong jaw. He was dressed in a pair of navy shorts and a white polo shirt. He had a wonderful smile.

"My name is Crane Maxxum. I'm from London, England. I'm staying at the hotel. And you?"

Callie cleared her throat and waited for the small shock of excitement to begin. It didn't. "Callie Masters. From Vancouver, Canada. Yes, I'm staying at the hotel. I don't believe there's too much choice in the matter."

Crane chuckled softly and shook her hand. "Well, Callie. Would you like to be my guest at supper tonight. I heard they have a terrific floor show."

Callie smiled sadly, ready to turn him down when a little voice inside reminded her she was supposed to be getting on with life. Anyway, sharing supper wasn't like committing yourself. "Yes, I'd like that." Callie took his hand and rose to her feet. "I'll meet you in the dining room at eight."

"That would be delightful. I look forward to an evening in the company of such a beautiful woman." He bowed very slightly and backed away as Callie headed for the hotel.

CALLIE TURNED this way and that in front of the mirror. Her dress was classy yet cool and somewhat sexy. For a moment she found herself wondering what Rock would have thought. She closed her eyes and sighed. She had to stop thinking about him. Downstairs was a very nice gentleman waiting for her company, and she was going to enjoy him if it killed her.

Crane rose as the waiter guided Callie to the candle-lit table in the corner. He took her hand and smiled warmly with appreciation. "You look magnificent. Like Snow White in your purity. White is becoming on you." He reached behind him and presented her with a branch of the most perfect dainty orchids in shades of pinks. "Pink for the delicacy of your skin. Please, sit." He pulled out her chair and began an evening of pampering. This man knew how to treat a woman.

Thus the next few days passed. Callie spent time with the gracious Crane during the daylight hours. They sailed and shopped, lunched and saw the sights together. They swam and talked of everything. And at night Callie lay awake thinking of Rock.

CALLIE SIPPED the last of the fruit drink Crane had ordered for her. "I had a wonderful time, Crane. I'm glad you invited me. I had planned a quiet evening, but I'm glad I came out with you."

"We couldn't have you spend your last evening on the island in your room. Would you like to walk?" he asked smoothly.

"Yes, that would be nice." Callie rose and pulled her lacy shawl over her bare shoulders. The new sundress she'd bought in town the other day was more daring than what she normally wore, but she'd fallen in love with the bright mauve, turquoise and pink print.

Crane escorted her onto the nearly deserted beach

where Callie had a moment of cautionary fear. She tamped it down, telling herself that she'd gotten to know this man and could trust him.

She was, after all, a woman who knew her own mind. She didn't have to walk too far, didn't have to do anything she didn't want to do.

They walked hand in hand in silence until they came to the waters edge. Callie removed her sandals and buried her toes in the wet warm sand.

"You are an unusual woman, Callie Masters," Crane observed. "I have never met a woman who talked so little about herself. I wish I could sneak into your head. I barely know anything about you. Do you lead a secret life?"

Callie stood absolutely still looking over the water to the horizon, afraid that if she moved she might break. She forced her thoughts to the reds and purples of the newly set sun as it stained the sky, but she saw none of the majesty. Tears welled in her eyes and she rapidly blinked them away. She wanted so much to enjoy this man. He was nice and very sweet, but he was not the man she wanted.

Crane turned her, held her in his arms and slowly lowered his head. Nothing happened. Oh, he kissed her. His lips brushed hers sweetly, but there were no explosions and no stars and no rushing heartbeat.

Crane pulled away and looked down at her. "Ah, a lost love," he said sadly, scooping a tear from her cheek. He took her very carefully into his arms. "Why you? Of all the women I've met, I wanted it to be you."

There was a long silence as Callie fought to gain control. His soft words almost undid her.

"If you still love him, then you must go back and fight for him. Otherwise, your life will be filled with grief and tears."

"Yes, I know," Callie whispered.

Taking her face between his hands, he gently kissed her lips. "My loss, angel. He must be a very special man. He's undoubtedly the luckiest, to have you."

It WAS DARK out there. Rock stared into the wilderness, then at the dying embers of the fire. Something inside him ached. The ache had pretty well been his companion since Callie had left. It was a hollow feeling he couldn't seem to fill no matter what he did, as if she had taken a physical chunk of him with her. He wondered if it would ever grow back. Somehow he had his doubts.

He lay on the groundsheet and crossed his legs, his arms folded under his head. Above, the stars twinkled in the dark sky. There were millions of them, but he still felt alone. That was why he had come here in the first place, to be alone. Not that he had to travel anywhere to do that—he was always alone these days.

She had done this to him. *How* was another one of those unanswered mysteries.

Damn it, he was in love with her. It was the only logical explanation and the only thing in this world he didn't want to believe.

How had it happened? He'd only made love to her

that one night...but in this case once was more than enough. Part of his soul—something vital—had been lost to her. Now he was left empty as she trotted off, happy to be rid of him.

Rock turned to his side clutching his chest. The ache remained in the empty spot where his heart should have been.

It was his own fault. He'd chased her away.

He conjured up the image of her lying in his arms in that small camper, her skin flushed from their loving, her eyes heavy with desire and her small hands comparing all the spots where he was hard and she was soft. His body reacted as a normal male body would at such erotic thoughts, not that it had far to go. He was always in a state of semi-arousal when he thought of Callie.

Something had to be done about this situation. He couldn't go on much longer this way. But how could he undo the damage he'd wrought to their relationship?

He had planned on getting himself a wife who would fill his bed and his home. Someone who would keep his house in order, give him children and comfort him at night. Lord, how he hated the sound of that—even to his own ears it sounded terrible. Suddenly it seemed more like he was looking for a combination brood mare and housekeeper than a wife. Why hadn't it occurred to him before that his ideal of a wife was biased and selfish beyond all reason? He could no more go out and marry some woman just to bear his kids and keep a house for him than he could marry Callie.

What did a man do when he loved a woman he couldn't have? What in hell's name was he going to do with this love he'd discovered for Callie Masters? What was love, anyway? Why had it belittled his father and taken his strength? Why did it take so much from a man and, apparently, so very little from a woman? Was there no explanation?

Rock closed his eyes and felt tears slide from his eyes into his hair. Tears, by God, tears! He hadn't cried in years, and he had no intention of giving in to them now. He turned over and willed himself to sleep.

After a while his body relaxed and Callie came into his mind to soothe and satisfy him. Rock sighed and wrapped himself around the fantasy of her.

CALLIE GRABBED one of the many boxes in her small office that sat waiting to be packed. She hated this job as much as she hated the one facing her at home. All she'd done for the past two weeks was pack, unpack and pack.

They had decided to open a western office and put her in charge of it. *They* had bought an office with an apartment up top for Callie. And she hadn't even been consulted. As if that wasn't enough, her father had put their house up for sale. He was moving into his new wife's home. Not only did she have to move because of the new office, but also because she wouldn't have anywhere to live.

Callie gritted her teeth. She didn't need this kind of aggravation at this point of her life, not after she had arrived home from her holiday more tired than before she'd gone.

It didn't help that Roarke McCall was praising and raving to everyone in their area about his house, and inquiries were pouring in. Nor did it help that the local press had done a photo layout of the two houses. She'd had to see the photo of the three brothers in front of Roarke's home. Her brother had thoughtfully had it enlarged and placed in the center of her desk to welcome her home.

Her life was falling apart because of the chauvinistic men in her life. Her father was too swept away with his new wife and selling the house from beneath her to see what was going on. Not that he would have helped her. He had agreed wholeheartedly with establishing the new branch. Her brothers were driving her crazy, and she felt as if the world was crowding in on her.

And through it all she was plagued with the very real fact that she still loved Rock and missed him like the dickens. She hated him for having made her love him like this.

Swiping away the tears that seemed to be a constant with her lately, she stuffed several folders into the box.

When Alex walked in the room and quietly shut the door behind him, she was still mopping up from the last spill of emotion. He dropped a sheaf of papers onto her desk and took her into his arms.

"Ah, dear little sister, cry it out. It's been a long time coming, hasn't it? Do you have to fight everything in your life? Must you even fight love when it's there at your fingertips?" He stroked her back gently and held her close as she soaked his shoulder. "If it makes you feel any better, he's as miserable as you."

Callie pulled away and took the offered hankie from Alex. "Who?"

Alex smiled warmly. "Rock McCall, that's who. That's who all these tears are for, isn't it?" He caught another tear on his finger.

Callie turned her back and cursed under her breath, but Alex heard her anyway. "Callie, must you? Look, why don't you just call him and talk it out? It's obvious you love him."

"I don't love him, I dislike him a great deal and I hate the things he did to me." She blew her nose into the hankie.

Alex went into his big-brother protector mode. "He didn't—"

"It's none of your business. I can take care of myself, you know," she said, negating the firmness in her voice by sniffling like a child.

"It's just that you threatened to go out and get pregnant. Oh, Lord, Callie. You're not?" He grasped her by the shoulders. His eyes had that desperate look to them.

"Oh, go to hell, Alex." She shrugged his hands off. "Get out of here, leave me alone. I have a lot of packing to do if I intend to leave tomorrow. And keep your mind out of the gutter." She pushed him from the room, not wanting to admit to him or even to herself what that long-past missed period meant. Perhaps it was better that she was moving away.

Even if it did mean living in Rock's backyard. Somehow she would survive.

11

"WHY THE HELL don't you go hunt Callie down and straighten this whole mess out?" Reese demanded.

Rock cast an icy stare toward his brothers. "What the hell does Callie have to do with this?" He held up the blue fiberglass cast that encircled his wrist.

"You know damn well I'm not talking about that," Reese burst out in a totally uncustomary way. "I'm sick of the cursing, grouching and complaining. The incessant pacing every damn night is just about driving me nuts. Why can't you just accept the fact that you love the woman and do something about it before you drive us all crazy? What the hell has you so scared?"

Rock flopped down at the end of the table and wrapped his one good hand around his mug of coffee. He gazed outside at the steadily falling rain. Autumn had set in, and the trees looked like wildfire, which only served to remind him how much he missed that fiery woman who still held control over his life. "I didn't ever want to love her. I still don't. Just be patient with me. It'll die out sooner or later. It has to, I'm not going to give in to it."

"What the hell does that mean?" Roarke demanded.

Rock didn't look at either of them. Instead he focused on the small picture that hung beside the back door. It was a faded snapshot of his father holding his mother. Their foreheads were pressed together and they were laughing about something private. They were so much in love that it showed as clearly as if the picture had been labeled Love. "I never wanted to love a woman like Dad loved Mom," he stated.

"What?" Roarke's head jerked up.

"I don't want to be trapped by love like Dad was trapped by Mom. She made him weak."

"Well, isn't that just the dumbest thing you ever heard." Roarke jumped to his feet and spun around. His fist crashed down on the table as his gaze swung from Rock to Reese and back. "This twit here thinks loving a woman makes you weak. Well, listen to me, boy, and listen good." He leaned over the table and met Rock's eyes with thunderous intent. "If I could ever be so lucky to find even a sliver of the type of love that Mom and Pop shared, I'd take it and treasure it for a lifetime. I'd nurture and pamper it every day of my life. I'd hold it close to my heart and never let go of it. Love like that comes along so very seldom, and when it does you grab on to it and let it take you. Hell, what do you think we were put on this earth for but for love and life?" Roarke's voice had calmed and his seriousness froze Rock to his chair in shock.

"In all my years I have watched friends of mine fall in love and stay together through some pretty rough times. The only way they managed to get by was because of the love they had between them. You may have thought Dad was weak because of the devotion and love he had for Mom, but that wasn't weakness."

He shook his head. "No, that was caring. That was living life to its fullest. That was happiness. I never knew another man as happy as our father, nor as contented. He would have been the first to admit that if it wasn't for Mom he'd never have been half the man he was. If you love Callie Masters the way you think Dad loved Mom, then you already know you aren't a complete man without her."

Roarke stopped and looked at his pale-faced brother. "And you will never be complete until she's with you forever. If you love her, Rock, quit being so stubborn and go claim her."

Rock thought of the terrible emptiness inside him and how it grew greater each and every day. He no longer had the will or desire to do anything. She filled his mind and, yes, his heart every minute of every day. He barely slept, and his appetite had all but disappeared. She had taken parts of him that he knew he'd never find if she didn't come back to him.

But it was hopeless. He'd said all those mean things to her. How could he ever expect her to forgive him? Closing his eyes, Rock felt the blanket of hopelessness smother all hope. Lord, he loved her more than his own life. Roarke was right—without her he would never be complete. What in heaven's name was he going to do?

Rock sighed heavily and shook his head. He couldn't meet his brother's eyes—his guilt and pain were too strong. "I can't. She can't possibly feel anything but hate for me at this point. I said too many things to hurt her. I chased her away. I guess I was scared of what I felt. Lord, the things I said to her, the pain I caused. How can I expect her to forgive me if I can't forgive myself?" He paced to the window and stared at the dark clouds. They echoed what he felt inside—dark and heavy with regret.

Reese spoke quietly from the other side of the room. "She'll forgive you. She loves you and has for a long time. She told me herself, after you went to the hospital in the summer. I thought by now you'd have figured that out."

Roarke added, "Her brother told me she's as miserable as you are. Go to her, Rock, before it's too late to patch up the wounds. You'll never find what you've lost without her by your side. I only wish I could be so lucky as to have fallen as hard as you."

Rock shook his head, but a small ray of hope was blossoming in his heart. Warmth filled him as he realized he had to go to Callie and explain. He had to have her in his life.

He loved her.

Something inside burst into light, and he accepted that she was his fate. She was his life. She was his love.

The first smile he'd managed to produce in a long while stretched across his face. It felt good. He looked from one brother to the other and laughed out loud with relief. "I guess I'd better pack up a few things and do some serious courting. I've got a wife to bring home. Guess I'll be the first to fulfill his end of the deal."

"Good luck," Roarke said, slapping his brother on the shoulder. Rock wiped away a stray tear as he slipped outside.

ROCK MCCALL was a big man. A man with purpose in his stride. Alex Masters knew who he was the minute he barged into his office.

Alex stood, offering his hand, then withdrew it when he saw that Rock's hand was in a cast. "Alex Masters, you must be Rockwell McCall."

"Rock McCall. I go by Rock."

"Right. Will you sit down, Rock?" Alex offered.

"No, thank you. I'm looking for Callie. Is she here?"

"Sorry, you just missed her. She's gone," Alex said, watching the cowboy before him with keen interest.

"Gone where?" Rock roared like a wounded lion.

"Calm down. She's moved out to our new office. In fact I'm surprised you hadn't heard about it. It's right in your neighborhood. She has an apartment above the office and should be getting settled in just about now." He glanced at his watch. "The movers left here at dawn this morning. Would you like her address?"

Rock sighed and wiped a large hand over his face. "Yes, please. Sorry I overreacted. I've been doing that a lot lately."

"It's all right, I understand how love is. It makes us irrational and stupid, but it's worth it." Alex laughed as he scribbled the address on an envelope.

Rock couldn't help but smile. "It's that obvious?"

Alex commiserated. "Yes, I too, have been there. You get better at handling it as time goes on. The desperation wears off after a while. Go to her, she needs you."

Rock took the envelope and thanked Alex as he crossed to the door. Alex's voice stopped him as he turned the handle. "If you ever hurt her again. I'll fix you but good."

Rock laughed. "Don't worry about me hurting her. She has more power to hurt me than I ever had to hurt her." He stopped and cleared his throat, but didn't look at Alex. "I love her. I'll never hurt her again. I hope that she'll strengthen me, make me a better man."

When Rock left the office, Alex picked up the phone and dialed Roarke. "Mission accomplished," he said, and was greeted by a low chuckle.

CALLIE HAD a hard time sleeping that night. Refusing to cry, she nuzzled into the pillow, but she was tired from unpacking and she was disappointed. For some fool reason she had thought maybe Rock would have caught wind of the move and come to her.

Why did she have to love him, anyway? She was exhausted by the effort of trying to forget him. And then there was this little secret she carried around inside her.

She hadn't allowed herself to acknowledge the tiny presence deep inside her body. Her missed period had turned into two missed periods. A simple home test had confirmed her suspicions, which meant there was two months of love growing beneath her heart. Two months since that wonderful night of passion she'd shared with Rock. Not until she had traveled today had she really thought about it. Now was the time to accept it. It didn't make sense to ignore something that she had wanted for so many years.

She lay back and placed her hands over the warm

spot between her hips. A baby... A tiny scrap of love left from that which they had shared. It was so ironic—she had been sent out to Blue Sky to prevent this exact thing from happening. But it had, as if somehow, some way fate had intervened.

Not that she regretted what had happened between her and Rock. It was just that she had always wanted to love someone big and strong with good values and a firm hold on life. She had wanted to share her life and raise a child or two with that man. She had found all those qualities in Rock, and she had the child, but she didn't have the man.

What a folly love is, she thought, taking and giving...confusing and needy. Callie drifted off to sleep. She'd deal with all of this tomorrow.

SHE WOKE to a pounding at her door. Although the apartment was on the second floor, the entryway was on the main floor at the bottom of the stairs. The pounding came again. Not only had it awakened her from a deep sleep, it also scared the devil out of her. Callie rolled from the bed and slipped to the kitchen to look down the stairwell.

Here she was, new in town. She knew no one, and someone was pounding on her door at midnight. And the only phone was downstairs in the office. She couldn't even call the police. For a moment she thought of Rock and wished he was here to help her, but that was just wishful thinking.

The pounding stopped, then became more insistent, and Callie gnawed her bottom lip trying to de-

cide what to do. She yelped as the door at the bottom
of the stairs gave way to a heavy blow.

Damn. She ducked into the bedroom and stood
shaking behind the closed door. What did she do
now? Well, what every other woman in this situation
would do...protect herself. But with what? She spotted the small foot-long souvenir bat a friend had
brought her from a baseball game. Grabbing it, Callie
stood behind the bedroom door, waiting as the
prowler thumped up the stairs, his footsteps getting
closer. Her heavy breathing froze as the handle on the
door turned slowly and opened. Callie winced and
gripped the bat a little tighter, holding it above her
head.

The stranger crept into the room and turned his
back to her, looking toward the mattress on the floor
that was her bed. He cursed.

Callie swung the bat down on the intruder's head.
He crumpled to the floor like a ton of bricks being
dumped.

Callie panicked as she stepped over the big body
toward the light. "Oh, my Lord." Had she recognized
that voice? Her hands and arms aching, she flicked on
the light and turned to find the one man with whom
she consistently made these errors...Rock McCall.

"Oh, Lord." Callie sank down beside his uncon-
scious form and cradled his head in her arms. "Oh,
Rock, darling. I'm sorry. I'll go get some help."

THIS WAS A DREAM, Rock was sure it was. Only a
dream could smell this good or feel so warm. No

voice could soothe him like Callie's did. And Callie was...well, she wasn't here.

He moved his head and pain sliced through him. He groaned. On second thought, perhaps Callie *was* around. If so, he had to talk to her. "Callie?"

"Yes. Oh, Rock. I'm sorry. I thought you were a prowler." She cried as she touched his chest and arm.

Another voice joined hers. "Stand back, Callie. Let the doctor finish his work." It was Reese.

"Reese, what are you doing..." Rock tried to move his hand but Roarke held it down. "Ouch. Damn it!"

"Lie still, Rock." Roarke's voice was added to the others. "Let the doctor finish with this last stitch and I'll let you up."

"Doctor? Callie, what have you done to me now?"

The room exploded with laughter. Rock grew more agitated as he tried to piece together what had happened. He had broken the lock on the door because Callie wasn't answering and he knew she was in there. He feared something terrible had happened to her. But when he'd arrived upstairs and gone to the only closed door and opened it, Callie wasn't in her bed. And then there was nothing.

Roarke released his arms and helped him roll over to sit on the edge of the mattress. Everything was blurry and wobbly, and Rock's stomach felt like curdled milk. He opened and closed his eyes several times. Roarke and the doctor stood hovering to the side. Callie was nestled into Reese's arms at the bottom of the bed. She was pale and dressed in a short blue robe. Anger and fury ripped through Rock, and he lunged from the bed toward Reese. "Why, you two-timing..."

Roarke and the doctor grabbed him and pulled him onto the bed. "Watch your wrist, boy! I guess he needs a shot to calm him down for the night, otherwise none of us is going to get any sleep tonight. Reese, come and hold him down for me." The doctor spoke in an exasperated tone.

"Oh, no, you don't, you double-crossing... She's mine! You know she's mine." Rock yelled, fought and bucked until he felt the needle poke his arm and the warmth travel upward. He relaxed, unable to fight the potent sedative.

"Yes, I know she's yours, and so does half the town now. Calm down and relax," Reese consoled his younger brother.

Rock turned to Reese and met his brother's eyes. "Why're ya holding my woman?" he asked, slurring.

"She was upset because she knocked you out. I was comforting her, that's all. Callie, come over here and straighten him out, will you?" Reese shook his head at the sorry sight his brother made.

Once Callie was at his bedside, the others left them alone to sort through the mess.

"Oh, Rock, I'm sorry, I didn't mean to hurt you. Please forgive me, love. I'm sorry. I love you." Her tears dampened Rock's cheek and he reached up to cradle her head on his shoulder.

"I love you, too, sweetheart," he murmured, then promptly dropped off to sleep.

Callie looked around the empty room, surprised to find herself alone with Rock. That was all right with her. He was her love, her man, the only one she wanted. She crawled in beside him and cuddled close, where she was meant to be. She slept deeply for the first time in weeks.

WHAT A DREAM, Rock thought. He was obviously recovering from one hell of a drunk. Here beside him was Callie, all soft and sweet, pressed up against him. She sighed and nestled closer, murmuring his name.

He opened his eyes and realized it was no dream, although he did have one hell of a headache. She *was* here beside him. Rock sighed heavily. What else could he expect? She was a jinx—where she was, trouble was. But he loved her, and that was all that mattered.

"Callie? Sweetheart?" Rock kissed her forehead gently and pulled her closer, if that was possible.

"Mmm." She moved away, then returned to the warmth of his arms. "Rock?" she murmured sleepily.

"I came to ask you to be my wife and love me forever. I want you to make me strong with your love. I love you...only you. Will you?"

This was something she didn't have to think about. "Yes, yes. I love you, Rock McCall. I love you."

"And I love you regardless of the stitches in my head, Jinx." He reached out to pull her into his arms and kissed her with all the love that he'd held back until now. He was at home at last.

"Mmm. Jinx, I almost lost you," Rock mumbled when he surfaced from the kiss they shared. He spoke in an intimate whisper. "I didn't want to love you. I was so frightened that I'd love you too much and it would take my strength away. I didn't understand that love really gave the strength and courage I thought weakened other men." He hesitated, pulling her closer into his arms. "I saw my daddy die trying to rescue my mother. He was so desperate that he might lose her, he lost his own life. And the last thing I remember him saying was that he'd rather die than live without her. I understand why he said that now, but back then I was too young and I thought he'd made a stupid choice to risk his life. But if I had to make the choice with you, I'd take the same one Daddy did back then. I've been so stupid."

"Not stupid. Just a little frightened or maybe confused. You had the good sense to fall in love with me. You were just frightened of a love that was so powerful and overwhelming. I was, too, for a while."

Rock wrapped his arms around Callie, feeling more contented than he had in years. "I can't think of anything that has run me over and knocked me around like you have. In fifty years I'll be able to tell our grandkids that their grandmother knocked me off my feet the first time I met her and had to hit me over the head to get me to marry her."

Callie smiled warmly. "I guess I should tell you that you'll be able to tell our child within a year."

Rock hesitated as he reached for his jeans and searched the pocket. "Child? Ours?" he asked softly.

Callie nodded, placing her hand on her still flat tummy.

Rock let out a huge breath. "Oh, sweet Jesus. I'm going to be a father. You...you're going to be a mother," he crowed. "Are you all right?"

Callie nodded, and Rock pulled her into his arms for a long soul-searching kiss. "I guess it's all the more reason I should give these to you." He grabbed his jeans and dug into the pocket then turned back to her. "Thank you, sweetheart. I'll never be able to thank you for everything you brought into my life. I love you so very much." He held out two small boxes, which he handed to her one at a time.

Callie almost cried when she opened the first. It contained a diamond surrounded by deep blue sapphires. Rock took it from the box and slid it onto her finger. "I love you. Marry me, Callie. Please." He bent his head and covered her mouth.

Callie nodded and tried to fight back the tears that welled in her eyes. They ran down her cheeks anyway.

Rock brushed away the tears and gently kissed her again, then lifted the lid of the second box and sat back to watch her reaction.

This time Callie threw back her head and laughed, not bothering to try and stop the tears. The box held a fine gold chain with a golden bell dangling from it. Rock fastened it around her neck and joined in her laughter.

"I warned you that this was needed long ago. But I'm giving it to you for a totally different reason than what I suggested before. I want you to wear this so I'll always know when you're nearby. I don't ever want to miss a chance to celebrate the love we've found. I love you, Callie, my sweet jinx."

Take 4 bestselling love stories FREE

Plus get a FREE surprise gift!

HARLEQUIN®

Temptation

It's a dating wasteland out there! So what's a girl to do when there's not a marriage-minded man in sight? Go hunting, of course.

Manhunting

Enjoy the hilarious antics of five intrepid heroines, determined to lead Mr. Right to the altar— whether he wants to go or not!

She's got a plan—to find herself a man!

Available wherever Harlequin books are sold.

DEBBIE MACOMBER

invites you to the

HEART OF TEXAS

Join Debbie Macomber as she brings you the lives
and loves of the folks in the ranching community
of Promise, Texas.

If you loved Midnight Sons—don't miss
Heart of Texas! A brand-new six-book series
from Debbie Macomber.

Available in February 1998
at your favorite retail store.

Heart of Texas by Debbie Macomber

Lonesome Cowboy	February '98
Texas Two-Step	March '98
Caroline's Child	April '98
Dr. Texas	May '98
Nell's Cowboy	June '98
Lone Star Baby	July '98

HARLEQUIN®

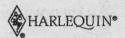

MURDER, BLACKMAIL AND LIES...

Suspicion

A young law clerk is killed. A high-priced call girl is strangled. Two men are accused of their murders. And defense attorney Kate Logan intends to prove their innocence—even though the evidence and witnesses say otherwise. With the help of homicide detective Mitch Calhoun, Kate discovers evidence suggesting that the two cases may be connected. But when her life and the life of her daughter are threatened, Kate and Mitch realize they have stumbled into a maze of corruption and murder...where no one is above suspicion.

CHRISTIANE HEGGAN

"A master at creating taut, romantic suspense." *—Literary Times*

Available January 1998
at your favorite retail outlet.

MIRA BOOKS

Look us up on-line at: http://www.romance.net

MCH305

Free Gift Offer

With a Free Gift proof-of-purchase
from any Harlequin® book, you can receive
a beautiful cubic zirconia pendant.

This stunning marquise-shaped stone is a genuine cubic
zirconia—accented by an 18" gold tone necklace.
(Approximate retail value $19.95)

Send for yours today...
compliments of &HARLEQUIN®

To receive your free gift, a cubic zirconia pendant, send us one original proof-of-
purchase, photocopies not accepted, from the back of any Harlequin Romance®, Harlequin
Presents®, Harlequin Temptation®, Harlequin Superromance®, Harlequin Love & Laughter®,
Harlequin Intrigue®, Harlequin American Romance®, or Harlequin Historicals® title
available at your favorite retail outlet, together with the Free Gift Certificate, plus a check or
money order for $1.65 U.S./$2.15 CAN. (do not send cash) to cover postage and handling,
payable to Harlequin Free Gift Offer. We will send you the specified gift. Allow 6 to 8 weeks
for delivery. Offer good until March 31, 1998, or while quantities last. Offer valid in the U.S.
and Canada only.

Free Gift Certificate

Name: _____

Address: _____

City: _____ State/Province: _____ Zip/Postal Code: _____

Mail this certificate, one proof-of-purchase and a check or money order for postage and
handling to: HARLEQUIN FREE GIFT OFFER 1998. In the U.S.: 3010 Walden Avenue, P.O.
Box 9071, Buffalo NY 14269-9057. In Canada: P.O. Box 604, Fort Erie, Ontario L2Z 5X3.

FREE GIFT OFFER   084-KEZ

ONE PROOF-OF-PURCHASE
To collect your fabulous FREE GIFT, a cubic zirconia pendant, you must include this
original proof-of-purchase for each gift with the properly completed Free Gift Certificate.

084-KEZR2